HOW TO DEFEAT A DEMON KING
IN TEN EASY STEPS

OTHER BOOKS BY ANDREW ROWE

The War of Broken Mirrors Series
Forging Divinity
Stealing Sorcery
Defying Destiny

Arcane Ascension Series
Sufficiently Advanced Magic
On the Shoulders of Titans
The Torch that Ignites the Stars
The Silence of Unworthy Gods

Weapons and Wielders Series
Six Sacred Swords
Diamantine
Soulbrand

The Lost Edge Series
Edge of the Woods

Death Game Quality Assurance

HOW TO DEFEAT A DEMON KING
IN TEN EASY STEPS

ANDREW ROWE

SAGA PRESS

LONDON NEW YORK TORONTO
AMSTERDAM/ANTWERP NEW DELHI SYDNEY/MELBOURNE

AN IMPRINT OF SIMON & SCHUSTER, LLC

1230 AVENUE OF THE AMERICAS, NEW YORK, NEW YORK 10020

For more than 100 years, Simon & Schuster has championed authors and the stories they create. By respecting the copyright of an author's intellectual property, you enable Simon & Schuster and the author to continue publishing exceptional books for years to come. We thank you for supporting the author's copyright by purchasing an authorized edition of this book.

No amount of this book may be reproduced or stored in any format, nor may it be uploaded to any website, database, language-learning model, or other repository, retrieval, or artificial intelligence system without express permission. All rights reserved. Inquiries may be directed to Simon & Schuster, 1230 Avenue of the Americas, New York, NY 10020 or permissions@simonandschuster.com.

This book is a work of fiction. Any references to historical events, real people, or real places are used fictitiously. Other names, characters, places, and events are products of the author's imagination, and any resemblance to actual events or places or persons, living or dead, is entirely coincidental.

Copyright © 2020 by Andrew Rowe
Previously published in 2020 by Andrew Rowe

All rights reserved, including the right to reproduce this book or portions thereof in any form whatsoever. For information, address Saga Press Subsidiary Rights Department, 1230 Avenue of the Americas, New York, NY 10020.

First Saga Press hardcover edition September 2025

SAGA PRESS and colophon are trademarks of Simon & Schuster, LLC

Simon & Schuster strongly believes in freedom of expression and stands against censorship in all its forms. For more information, visit BooksBelong.com.

For information about special discounts for bulk purchases, please contact Simon & Schuster Special Sales at 1-866-506-1949 or business@simonandschuster.com.

The Simon & Schuster Speakers Bureau can bring authors to your live event. For more information or to book an event, contact the Simon & Schuster Speakers Bureau at 1-866-248-3049 or visit our website at www.simonspeakers.com.

Interior design by Erika R. Genova

Manufactured in the United States of America

1 3 5 7 9 10 8 6 4 2

Library of Congress Control Number: 2025939955

ISBN 978-1-6682-0942-4
ISBN 978-1-6682-0944-8 (ebook)

This one is dedicated to all the people out there trying to save our world, in any way they can. Thank you to all the doctors, engineers, scientists, teachers, and other wonderful human beings who work to save lives or make our existence better.

CONTENTS

STEP ONE:
Be the Legendary Chosen Hero — 1

STEP TWO:
Unlock Your Latent Heroic Power — 11

STEP THREE:
Obtain the Hero's Sword — 21

STEP FOUR:
Find the Most Powerful Monsters Available — 33

STEP FIVE:
Defeat the Deadly Monsters to Increase Your Abilities — 51

STEP SIX:
Use the Traditional Steps to Defeat Each Dungeon — 63

STEP SEVEN:
Wait, You Forgot to Recruit Loyal Companions, Do That — 95

STEP EIGHT:
Okay, Now Clear the Remaining Dungeons in the Proper Order — 121

STEP NINE:
Prepare for the Final Battle — 165

STEP TEN:
Defeat the Demon King — 179

STEP ELEVEN:
There Were Only Ten Steps, What Went Wrong? — 203

EPILOGUE:
Find a New Goal — 217

Afterword — 223
Acknowledgments — 229

STEP ONE

BE THE LEGENDARY CHOSEN HERO

FATHER ALWAYS TOLD ME that true heroism was when someone fought for what was right, regardless of the risk to themselves.

But Father was wrong.

True Heroism was a passive skill only available to the Hero class, unlocked at forty-second level.

Unfortunately, I wasn't a Hero. There wasn't much chance that I ever could have been, really. For whatever reason, Hero was an advanced class that only Farmers and Orphans could unlock, at least as far as anyone could tell me.

This was unfortunate, because the world really needed a Hero, even if most people weren't willing to admit it.

The year was 4423D. The twenty-third year in the reign of the resurrected Demon King.

Tradition held that the Demon King would expand his power for a hundred years after his rebirth. Only then would the Hero be reborn.

This had happened dozens, maybe hundreds of times. History generally remembered the great Heroes based on their most famous accomplishments. We called them the First Hero, the Speedy Runner Hero, the Faerie Harem Hero, and so on.

They always had brave companions, too. The most notable were their faeries—the Fire Faerie, the Sword Faerie, and more infamous ones like the Faerie Who Failed and the traitorous Fallen Faerie.

Historically, the Hero was usually born just in time to turn the war around, with half of the planet under the Demon King's control. Maybe a little more, a little less, depending on how ambitious the current Demon King was.

This time around, things had gone a little differently. A major human nation had sold out to the Demon King more or less instantly, and then marched with his armies to wipe out the neighboring nations of dwarves and elves. From there, they'd pressed on further, taking more soldiers from the survivors of nations they burned and enslaved.

The result?

We had seventy-seven years before the revival of the Hero, and more than half the world had already been taken.

If we waited for the coming of the Hero, there wouldn't be much of a world left for him to save.

Fortunately, I had a plan.

When I was young, I hoped to earn a class like Warrior or Barbarian. Who didn't want to hit people with a giant sword? And they had some great advanced classes, too.

But I wasn't born particularly strong. Or fast. Or, if I'm being honest, talented with weapons.

Unlocking classes had certain requirements. They weren't always things you had to accomplish, at least for basic classes—losing your parents at a young enough age could get you the Orphan class. In spite of the humble-sounding name, it's one of the strongest classes to start with. Enough so that some people might take extreme steps to try to earn it.

No, I didn't do anything dark and murderous to get a class like that. I like my parents. I did, however, briefly ask Mom to disinherit me so I could get a shot at unlocking it.

"No, dear. I'm not going to disown you and put you out on the streets to get a class. That would be terribly irresponsible."

"But Mommmm, it probably wouldn't take more than a few days for me to be eligible."

Mom gave me a withering look, folding her arms. "Absolutely. Not. And I will hear nothing more of the matter."

A few minutes later, my next conversation began with, "So, Daddy, I was wondering if you'd be willing to disown me a little."

He thought it was funnier, but he was similarly unconvinced.

Much of my childhood went like that.

I remember hearing a lot of things like:

"No, dear, I don't believe that giving you a miniature village and burning it down would count as a tragic backstory."

"Absolutely not, sweetie. We are not renaming you 'Hero' to try to fool the goddesses. No reasonable person would be fooled by that, and the goddesses certainly wouldn't be either."

"We are not buying a farm to get you the Farmer class. When you're old enough, if you want to go work on a farm, you can do that."

"You are most definitely not the missing child of a deposed royal bloodline, and we are not spreading rumors to that effect to try to get you a 'Secret Princess' class. I'm not even sure that's a class. I can't see why it would be."

"No, dear, I don't believe declaring our house a 'kingdom' would earn you the normal 'Princess' class, either."

They actually humored me and tried that one, declaring loudly the founding of "Our Housia" to the world. Predictably, nothing happened. I pushed for them to get some paperwork signed to authenticate our newly founded kingdom, but that was apparently a step too far.

You'd think I'd be disappointed by all that, but really, it just gave me fuel for more ideas. And in spite of many false starts, I eventually found one that worked. For certain values of "worked," anyway.

From the age of nine onward, I wore a backpack all the time. For eight years, I hauled things around for friends, family, and eventually as a part-time job, until finally I unlocked the right class.

While that might sound like something you'd do to unlock an Explorer class—and, indeed, there is one with similar requirements—I was shooting for something a lot less popular.

The illustrious Bag Mage class.

No, not Blue Mage. Bag Mage.

Doesn't sound very impressive, does it?

Bag Mages generally have one function in society—hauling goods long distances. They often serve as assistants to Merchants. Some Merchants even multi-class into it, if they're too poor to afford a Bag Mage of their own... but most of them won't admit to it.

Nobles will often employ a Bag Mage or two to haul their stuff around when they go on vacations or that sort of thing. Umbrellas, tents, all those things you might expect a pack animal to carry... Bag Mages.

If you're thinking that sounds like a cross between a wizard and a mule, you have the right idea about where we tend to fit into society.

By the way, Bag Mage isn't even the easiest magic-using class to unlock. I could have gotten a traditional Fire Mage class by starting a bunch of fires, for example, in a much smaller time frame. Similarly, all I would have needed for a Life Mage class was to spend a lot of time mending plants, animals, and people.

So, why'd I want to be a Bag Mage, when I could have worked to get something more impressive sounding with much less effort?

Well, Bag Mages have one particularly useful ability—Inventory—the ability to put something they're touching into an extradimensional space, then retrieve it later.

Inventory has a number of limitations. Every Bag Mage has a maximum capacity for their Inventory. They have a limited number of slots, and each slot has a capacity in terms of the size and mass of an object that can be stored within it. A novice Bag Mage has such a small Inventory that it barely has any use. At the start, the most I could store was four large rocks, one in each of my four Inventory slots.

Fortunately, I only needed to store one thing in order to get my plan started.

Upon obtaining my class, I was finally ready to test the first stage of my plan. For this, I had to travel to the Sword Shrine.

The Sword Shrine was the location that housed the legendary Hero's Sword, one of the only weapons capable of harming the Demon King. The blade was plunged into a metal platform encrusted with divine enchantments designed to only allow a True Hero to draw it.

In the days of ancient history, the Sword Shrine was a place of great reverence, attended to by priests and serving as a quiet place of prayer and contemplation.

Currently, it was a popular tourist destination. The kingdom charged a small fee for anyone to enter and try to draw the sword—which was, of course, supposed to be impossible for anyone other than the Hero.

Kids loved it. My coin purse hated it.

But on the positive side, it gave me a chance to test my plan without having to do anything too shady, like sneaking in during the middle of the night. (I wasn't above doing that sort of thing, but I was grateful I didn't have to resort to such tactics . . . at least for the moment.)

I paid the fee and waited in line.

In front of me, I watched numerous others attempt to draw the legendary blade. The sword's crystalline hilt shimmered brightly, and the pommel jewel was breathtaking. (I wondered absently if anyone had ever tried to pry it off.)

The blade was the most beautiful part of all, with silvery-white metal that glimmered with divine power. Even at a glance, I could tell there was something wondrous about it. It was the type of shimmer and glow that captivated my imagination.

I could see myself wielding it proudly, defying the Demon King and striking him down.

Ahead of me, several small children seemed to share the same notion. I was mildly embarrassed, but still determined.

A huge guy walked up to the pedestal, gripped the blade tightly, and drew some attention from the crowd. He braced himself and yanked on the hilt, lightly at first. When the sword didn't budge, he pulled harder, gripping with two hands and straining with effort.

"Activate Strength of Steel!"

There was a gasp of astonishment from the crowd as his skin shifted to a metallic color and sheen. He'd activated a skill—one of the abilities granted by a class. From the look of him and the name of the skill, I was guessing he was a Blacksmith or something similar, and accustomed to working with metal.

With his body reinforced by a powerful skill like that, I bet he could have cracked ordinary stone or metal with his bare hands. But this was no ordinary blade, and the enchantments that held it were divine. It would take more than brute strength to tear it free.

Stronger people had tried and failed.

I gave him a nod of approval, though, even as his skill ended and he turned away in failure, allowing the next person to step up to the pedestal. His thought process was not dissimilar to my own, even if he'd taken a more direct approach than I intended to.

Minutes passed. I waited my turn, feeling my shoulders tighten and my stomach churn.

Could this possibly work?

Was I a fool for even trying?

With desperate hope and determination, I suppressed my anxiety and stepped up to the platform.

I rested my hands on the grip of the sword, imagining the struggles of Heroes long ago.

And with a word, I pronounced my intent.

"Inventory."

There was a brief shimmer from the blade, and then . . .

```
[Your Inventory skill level is too low to store this item.]
```

The message appeared in the midst of my vision. It wasn't one I'd seen before, but I understood the meaning.

I had failed.

But in spite of that, I felt my lips curl up in a smile.

I released the grip of the sword and made my way out of the Sword Shrine.

Skill levels could be earned.

Now, I had work to do.

STEP TWO

UNLOCK YOUR LATENT HEROIC POWER

IN ORDER TO IMPROVE my Inventory's functionality, I had to make use of it. That's how skills tend to work in general—use them enough and they get better. Use it a whole bunch and it might even unlock new skills, or improve into an advanced skill if it reaches the maximum skill level.

Notably, skill levels increase independently of your overall personal level. They're purely use-based.

For example, a Fire Mage who sits around in town and lights things on fire can increase their Fire Magic skill. This is, however, relatively slow for a few reasons. First, because skills increase much more slowly if they do not have a valid target. For Fire Magic, that means the Fire Mage would have to actually burn things. And when you burn things that aren't yours, that's arson, kids.

Second, unless you're doing some really good arson—meaning burning high-level stuff—raising a skill is a slow process. The higher level your target for a skill, the faster your skill increases.

This is why most adventurers raise their attack-focused skills by fighting monsters; they can do so without having to worry about being arrested.

(Sparring works to some degree, but just hitting someone with fire doesn't get you much of a reward unless they're significantly hurt... and that gets awkward. Anyway, I digress.)

The third problem is Fire Magic uses mana, a limited resource. Everyone has a little bit of mana flowing in their body. It's an ephemeral power that is used to power spells and skills, with each consuming a different amount of mana. Generally, the higher the level of a spell or skill, the more mana it consumes.

Using too much mana causes exhaustion. Eventually, if you run out entirely, you simply stop being able to use spells and skills until you rest and recover.

If I'd started out as a Fire Mage, I might have been able to throw three or so fire spells before I had to rest for a significant period of time. A higher-level Fire Mage would have more mana to work with, and thus be able to cast more spells... but actually increasing my level as a Fire Mage would require going out and fighting monsters. Fighting monsters when you can only cast three spells at a time is, of course, super dangerous—and also extremely tedious.

My dear, sweet Inventory didn't have those problems.

Any object that I wanted to put into my Inventory was a valid target for raising my skill.

And Inventory didn't cost any mana.

Putting items into my Inventory was nearly instant, and so was taking them out.

You probably see where this is going.

Each day and night after unlocking the class, whenever I had free time, I'd sit down and practice.

"Inventory."

A shimmering space would appear in front of me, displaying glittering symbols representing the items in my Inventory's space.

If I wanted to add an item to my inventory, I needed to touch it and speak the appropriate phrase. If I wanted to remove an item,

HOW TO DEFEAT A DEMON KING IN TEN EASY STEPS

I could either speak the appropriate phrase or press on the symbol corresponding to that item.

"Remove rock."

A rock appeared in my hand, and the rock symbol disappeared from my vision.

"Add rock."

The rock vanished, and the symbol reappeared.

```
[Your Bag Magic skill level has increased to 2.]
```

I laughed. It may have been a slightly maniacal laugh.

I am not ashamed.

My parents may have given me some worried looks, though.

"Remove rock."

"Add rock."

And so I continued.

Every time my Bag Magic skill increased, my number of Inventory slots increased. With a skill level of 2, I now had eight slots available.

I experimented with many other mundane objects around the household, both to alleviate my boredom and to try to determine what would increase my skill level the fastest.

My parents were somewhat confused by my hobby, but supportive.

"You need to take notes if you're going to be testing your skill gains," Father explained to me. "Here." He pushed over a quill and parchment. "As soon as you get to your next skill level, start counting."

"I'm already counting," I complained. "In my head. I have literally nothing better to do."

"Take notes," he insisted. "A pattern will most likely emerge. From there, we can get into efficiency testing."

I nodded to him.

Mother was a Merchant, and Father was a retired Scholar. Mother made the real money for the family, but Father did the bookkeeping—and he was good at it. He always had a head for numbers, and I'd like to think I inherited just a bit of it. Enough to understand his idea and put it into practice, at least.

As I continued the process, I followed his advice. I took meticulous notes on the number of times I needed to open my Inventory and use it before increasing my skill, and which item I'd used for that particular skill level.

The goal was simple enough—figure out if storing some items would increase my skill level faster than storing others. If I had some kind of skill for monitoring my progress between levels, it would have been a lot easier... but I didn't have anything that did that.

Now, if it always required a static amount of work to go up a level, this would have been relatively simple. Sadly, skills don't work that way. The amount of practice it takes to increase a level naturally goes up from one level to the next, and because the gods are vicious things, the rates of skill advancement aren't always consistent from skill to skill.

Thus, to determine the efficiency of individual items, I first had to test the same item across multiple skill levels to try to determine the approximate level curve. By that, I mean adding and removing the same rock over and over and checking how many repetitions it took to increase my skill level from 2 to 3, 3 to 4, etc.

That took a while.

After that, I got into testing the efficiency of different item types.

Some of the most obvious things to test would have been objects of extraordinary value, like bars of gold or legendary magical relics. Sadly, my parents were fresh out of both, so I stuck with the basics.

I tried smaller rocks (less efficient than the same large one I'd been using, but only if they were really small); keys (20 percent more efficient than rocks); coins (efficiency based on the metallic content, with silver weirdly being more efficient than gold); knives (even more efficient than coins); and a bunch of other random household items.

After that, I got into some more esoteric stuff.

"Add bag."

I was thrilled to find that I could store containers that contained other items in my Inventory, and apparently, they only took up a single "slot."

Unfortunately, in terms of my skill progression, storing a bag only seemed to "count" the bag itself—not the contents. So, storing a bag filled with coins wouldn't give me dozens of times more skill credit than storing a single coin. It was a shame, but good to know.

"Add water."

I was surprised to find that I could store liquid without it being in a container. I just put my hand into a bucket and a small amount of water vanished, which I could then remove from my Inventory at any time.

I didn't know if that would ever actually be useful, but it was interesting, at least.

"Add book."

Books were the strangest; they had different storage values on a per-book basis, which didn't appear to be based on the weight of the book.

I tried writing some things myself on parchment to see if I could figure out the efficiency of notes with individual letters (such as an empty page, or a page with the letter *A* written all over it, or a page with legible writing, or a page covered with ink), but I couldn't find any difference among those. I wasn't sure why, but I suspected it had something to do with individual pages being too small of a sample.

Throughout the process, I unlocked a number of Inventory-related skills.

```
[Your Bag Magic skill level has increased to 20.]
[You have learned the Improved Inventory Capacity skill.]
```

That skill drastically increased the size and mass of objects I could put into single Inventory slots. That was extremely useful, because while my number of slots had increased in a seemingly linear fashion with each level, my capacity per slot had only been increasing very slowly up until that point. I'd been able to store slightly larger rocks with each level, but I hadn't figured out a formula for it.

Anyway, with Improved Inventory Capacity, I had more options. I tested things like larger rocks and some metal pots and pans, but nothing turned out to be much more efficient for skill gains. Object size impacted skill gain rate a little, but not much. I tried some larger and more esoteric stuff after that, like storing walls, but...

HOW TO DEFEAT A DEMON KING IN TEN EASY STEPS

[Error: Cannot be stored.
Object is above maximum capacity.]

Unfortunate, but at least I could store more water in a single slot, or things like an entire backpack.

[Your Bag Magic skill level has increased to 50.]
[You have gained the Mental Inventory Activation skill.]

That was an interesting one; it let me open and close my Inventory or add and remove items just by thinking about it.

I tried testing if that changed the rate at which my skills increased, but it didn't seem to.

I went back to saying things aloud after that, at least for the most part. I was just too used to it.

Eventually, Mom loaned me her wedding ring.

That changed everything.

Thanks. I love you, Mom. And I owe you many, many thanks for the time you saved me on leveling up.

The wedding ring proved to be forty-five times more efficient than my dear, sweet, and reliable testing rock. It was also nearly ten times more efficient than the next-best thing I'd found, which was a fancy kitchen knife.

I think she was concerned about me losing it from time to time, but as long as I only used it while I was at home, she tolerated it.

And with that, I had everything I needed.

"Inventory. Remove wedding ring."

"Add wedding ring."

[Your Bag Magic skill level has increased to 75.]

[You have gained Superior Inventory Capacity skill.]

I still couldn't store walls, sadly, but I found myself capable of storing entire drums of water in one Inventory slot after that.

I kept going.

It took an entire year of spending hours and hours each day, but eventually, I reached the message I'd been striving for since the beginning.

[Your Bag Magic skill level has increased to 100.]
[You have gained the Ultimate Inventory Capacity skill.]

That was impressive in itself. Ultimate Inventory Capacity increased the amount of mass I could store in a single Inventory by a factor of ten. I was curious if I could store an entire house now, but my parents (barely) convinced me not to test that on our home.

That wasn't even the most important thing I'd earned, though. Not by a long shot.

A second message had displayed in my mind, one I'd only dreamed of seeing.

[Your Bag Magic has improved into the advanced skill Dimensional Magic.]

Perfect.

Now, it was about time I got myself a sword.

STEP THREE

OBTAIN THE HERO'S SWORD

AFTER RETURNING MY MOTHER'S wedding ring and giving her my eternal gratitude, I was ready to get started on my next test.

Along with Dimensional Magic, I had unlocked a single spell—Blink.

Blink was a short-distance teleportation spell that could be used on myself, any object of reasonable size I touched, or another person. I could also use it on myself and up to two other people at the same time, as long as we were in physical contact. Oh, and just to be clear, people were transported with whatever they were carrying. Teleporting people out of their clothes was a funny idea but not actually how the spell worked.

The main disadvantage of Blink was the range—it only could go about fifty feet, and it required a clear line of sight to the destination. I presumed that would be improved somewhat as I increased my Dimensional Magic skill, but likely not enough to ever be used as a long-distance travel spell. I'd probably have to unlock higher-level spells for that sort of thing.

It also cost mana to use, which I had very little of, since I was only first level. After testing it, I determined I had enough mana to use Blink a total of three times before I found myself completely exhausted and needed to rest.

If I tried to use Blink a fourth time, it failed outright, and I saw a message that said:

```
[You have insufficient mana to use this spell.]
```

I spent one day practicing with Blink, just to be safe. Doing that, as well as storing more things, didn't raise my Dimensional Magic skill at all. I wasn't too worried, though—increasing Dimensional Magic wasn't my priority.

I headed back to the Sword Shrine, nervously practicing storing things in my Inventory the whole journey. It only took me about a day to get there—my hometown wasn't far from the capital, Sovereign's Peak, where the Sword Shrine was located.

I paid the entrance fee, stood in line, and gripped the sword.

Please, please work.

"Inventory. Add Hero's Sword."

The blade of the sword flashed with bright light.

A message flashed in my vision too fast to process, and then I was surrounded by darkness.

The first thing I did was panic, which I think is pretty understandable, since I couldn't breathe.

The fact that I couldn't see my surroundings was pretty bad, too, but breathing is even more important.

It was cold, too. Oppressively cold. Numbness was rapidly spreading across my skin, and that same cold was rapidly flowing up my nose as I tried and failed to draw in breath.

I choked on the lack of air.

I flailed around for a moment, and my arm hit something hard. I could feel something, at least. That pain gave me the slightest bit of focus.

My hand moved, gripping the object, and I recognized it instantly. I'd stored it thousands upon thousands of times, after all.

My rock.

After a moment of confusion, I understood the void around me.

I opened my mouth, feeling frigid air enter, and spoke into the oppressive dark.

"Remove all Inventory."

Even as my throat froze, I felt something shift, and then the blessed light and warmth of the world returned.

I found myself back in the Sword Shrine, collapsed in front of the pedestal. I heard a murmur from the crowd around me.

I coughed and choked. I barely remember the next few minutes as people rushed around me.

Fortunately, among the priests at the shrine, at least a handful of them were still actual practitioners of divine magic.

I felt someone's warm hand on my forehead and heard a man's voice say, "Lesser Heal."

That warmth spread across my body. It was a blissful sensation, too perfect to bear after the harrowing ordeal I'd just gone through.

That, at least, is my best explanation for why I lost consciousness a few moments later.

I woke in an unfamiliar bed, too tired and weak to even panic at that fact.

Blearily, I opened my eyes and processed the world around me.

There was a man sitting in a chair next to me, wearing the traditional robes of a White Mage. He looked to be about my age, with dark skin and a distinctive scar over his right eye. He was asleep, at least until the moment I sat up.

"Wha... huh?" He wiped a bit of drool off his lips as he woke, then processed his own surroundings as I did.

I was in a small private chamber with stone walls on all sides, a large wooden door, and a stained glass window depicting four of the First Hero's companions in battle against the four generals of the Demon King. It was traditional for a Hero's companions to match themselves against each of the Demon King's Generals, one at a time, for reasons I could never fully understand.

From that, I put together my likely location. I felt a bit chagrined, but it was better to be in the Sword Shrine than in some random guy's bedroom.

"You're awake!" the man proclaimed, brightening at the sight of me. "Oh, you probably shouldn't sit up so fast, though. You're probably going to need to take some time to heal."

From the way my head was spinning, I had to agree. I groaned. "Mom is going to be pissed."

The robed man gave me a sympathetic smile. "Is there someone we should be contacting on your behalf, mayhap?"

"My parents know I'm here." I sighed. "I just... really was hoping it would work this time."

He raised an eyebrow at me. "This time?"

"I tried using my Inventory skill on the sword before, but I wasn't high enough level for it to even register. Now, apparently my skill level was high enough, but it went even worse. Must have triggered some kind of magical defense on the stone or the sword."

"Oh dear, yes. Perhaps you weren't thinking about Spell

Reflection? It's one of the Hero's Sword's iconic characteristics."

I sighed. I'd known that the Hero's Sword could reflect nearly all forms of magic. It was legendary for being able to reflect the Demon King's energy balls, after all. But I didn't think that would extend to something as innocuous as storing it in my Inventory.

It was only then that I was able to recall and process the message that I'd seen in my vision before I passed out.

[Your Inventory spell has been reflected.]

Oops.

"Well, that wasted quite a bit of time, then." I rubbed my throat, which still ached in spite of the healing. "Thanks for healing me. That was you, right?"

He nodded. "It's my job. Well, one of my jobs. You'd be surprised how many people hurt themselves trying to get the sword. At least you didn't use attack magic—that can make a real mess." He reached out with a hand. "I'm Ken. Ken Sei."

"Yui Shaw." I shook his hand. "Sorry to cause you trouble."

Ken laughed. "Ah, it's nothing! In fact, that was the most interesting thing that's happened here in years. Sure, people try to blow up the altar now and again, but I've never seen someone try a skill and simply vanish before. Very few people make a sincere effort to try unusual approaches like you did."

I gave him a weak smile. "Thanks, I guess. I guess I'll get started on plan B as soon as I'm healed."

"Plan B? I hope that doesn't involve a hammer and chisel."

I snorted. "No, no. I'm going to try my Blink spell next, but I don't think that'll work, either. Then from there, I'll give up on the sword for a while and try other things. I'll circle back around when I'm higher level and have more options."

"You seem very invested in the idea of pulling out this sword." Ken frowned. "Why is that?"

"I can't just wait for some Hero to show up and save the world." I took a breath. "I can't just wait and watch while the world burns around me. There's no telling how much will be left when the Hero rises. And even when he does arrive, he could fail. It's happened."

"Twice, that we know of." Ken nodded. "The Bad End Hero, who was defeated by the Demon King when his faerie companion—the Fallen Faerie—betrayed him. And then there was Water Temple Hero, who was supposedly the most powerful Hero of all time, but disappeared into the Water Temple, never to return."

I should have expected someone who worked at the Sword Shrine to be well-versed in the legends of the Hero. "Yeah. What if it happens again? With the rate that the Demon King's armies are moving..."

"He has a chance to succeed this time and completely wipe out humanity." Ken nodded. "I know. I agree with you."

"You do?" I blinked.

"Indeed. But there's nothing to be done." He shook his head sadly. "Alas and alack, none can challenge the Demon King without the Hero. So it is written, and so it shall always be."

"Is that really such a certainty, though?" I frowned. "I mean, haven't some other adventurers gotten close to beating him?"

"There are scattered tales, to be certain. But I'm afraid neither of us is quite the right person for the job. We're dressed entirely wrong for it, for one."

"What does that have to do with it?" I asked.

HOW TO DEFEAT A DEMON KING IN TEN EASY STEPS

"It's well-known that the Hero must always wear a green tunic," Ken said. "It's one of his most iconic characteristics. And neither of us is properly dressed for such a role."

"...I could buy a different outfit?" I offered. "But wait, hold on. No. That clearly can't be a relevant problem."

"You'd be surprised how important an outfit can be. And beyond that, equipment. Do you have bombs? A bow? Magic arrows? A harmonica?"

"...No? But wait, no. I can see why bombs and arrows might be helpful, but why in the world would I need a harmonica?"

Ken raised an eyebrow. "To play the sacred melodies, obviously. Haven't you heard the legends at all?"

"Some of the Heroes played those songs, but not all of them. And besides, I was really planning to circumvent a lot of that."

Ken patted me on the knee. "I'm sure you were, dear. But there are reasons why the Hero must do the things he does. It's tradition, you know."

"The Demon King seems to be ignoring tradition himself. He's conquering far faster this time."

"Indeed. Very rude of him, I must say." Ken shook his head. "It's like he has no standards at all!"

I sighed. "Right. Don't you think we should, you know, maybe do something about that?"

Ken hesitated. "I...don't know. That sounds an awful lot like breaking from tradition."

"I'm going to be honest—I'm not that worried about it. I'd rather, you know, actually save people?"

Ken lowered his head. "I...suppose. You're not the only one who feels that way. I've seen other adventurous types who have said the same. Many powerful adventurers come by and try to claim the sword, desperate to make a difference. I've seen people try dozens of clever things. Trying to dispel the runes, trying to reshape the platform... someone even changed their name to 'Hero' to try to trick the sword that way."

I snorted. "That's a good one. I should meet that guy."

"Didn't work, obviously, but there have been many good efforts." He frowned. "If the goddesses do not will it, what chance does any of us have to succeed?"

"I don't know," I admitted. "But all I can do is try. There's no harm in trying to save the world, is there?"

"Well, not unless you break something important," he pointed out. "Please don't break anything important?"

"Can't promise anything." I smiled. "But you know, if you're worried about me breaking things, you could go with me."

Ken frowned. "I'm not certain what use I would be. I have very few skills, aside from healing magic, an impeccable fashion sense, and prodigious skill at swordplay."

I stared at him. "... What was that last part again?"

"Oh, I'm rather good with color coordination, if I say so myself. I very nearly took a level in Fashionista, but—"

"No, the other last part. Aren't you supposed to be a priest?"

Ken smiled. "Ah, I suppose I didn't introduce myself properly. I am a priest, at least in profession. But that's not my class." He shifted so I could see that on the side of his robes he had a belt. "I have a somewhat unusual class. It came from being raised at the Sword Shrine, and training here in both holy magic and the use of swords."

"Unusual class?"

He rested a hand on the hilt at his side. "Indeed. They call me a Sword Saint."

That night, Ken helped me down the stairs. I was a little wobbly on my feet, but determined not to waste the evening.

Then, with his assistance, I tried a few things.

"Blink."

The sword shimmered brightly when I cast the spell on it, then I found myself teleported in the opposite direction of where I'd intended to transport the sword.

I frowned, but it wasn't the worst possible scenario. I could have ended up in an endless suffocating void again, or maybe teleported inside the floor.

That would have been awkward.

After that, it was time to test the pedestal. Even if the sword had spell reflection, that didn't mean the pedestal itself did.

"Inventory. Add pedestal."

```
[The target has resisted your Inventory spell.]
```

I wrinkled my nose.

"Inventory."

I repeated that a hundred times. The pedestal resisted me every time.

Still, resistance wasn't immunity. Maybe if I got my Dimensional Magic skill high enough, I'd be able to make it work.

Next, I tried to teleport the pedestal.

"Blink."

[Invalid target.]

Hm. That's frustratingly vague. I wonder if it's because the pedestal is attached to the ground?

Unfortunately, I didn't have enough experience with using Blink to fully understand its limitations yet. The message itself wasn't very clear, either. For the moment, the important part was that it hadn't worked, and that it hadn't mentioned anything about my skill level being too low. That meant that it was unlikely to be a skill-related problem, and thus, I probably wouldn't be able to get it to work in the future. I'd have to keep looking for other options to test.

After my failures, I watched Ken make his own efforts.

"Great Lia, high above us in the Kingdom of the Sky, I beseech you. Please give me your guidance, and show me the righteous path. For I, your humble servant, seek only to end the darkness that encroaches upon this land."

He placed his hands on the hilt.

"Bless." He cast the spell on himself, making a soft golden glow play across his skin. "Lesser Strength."

Then he pulled on the hilt.

As expected, it didn't budge.

I waited a few minutes politely while he prayed silently, then helped me back up the stairs.

"It was a good effort," I said to him.

"Agreed," he replied. "So, what is the next step of your plan?"

"This may sound like an odd question... but do you have any idea where we can find some slimes?"

STEP FOUR

FIND THE MOST POWERFUL MONSTERS AVAILABLE

KEN DID NOT, IN fact, know where to find slimes. He did, however, know how to locate the local Adventurer's Guild.

There, we were directed at the counter to a grizzled veteran. She was over six feet tall, battle scarred, and wore some kind of unidentifiable animal hide. On her back, she wore a huge axe made out of some kind of crystal.

I liked her immediately.

"Excuse me." I walked over to her. "Can I ask you a few questions?"

"Already are, little one. What can Gretta help you with?" She gave me a broad smile, exposing teeth that were just a little too sharp.

"We were hoping to find a place with slimes?"

"Slimes? Is common monster. Go anywhere." She waved a hand. "Forest, hills, wizard lair . . . many slimes." Gretta nodded, mostly to herself.

"Is there a place where we can find slimes in a high concentration, without a lot of other monsters?" Ken asked.

"Why? Is slime bounty season again?" She frowned. "No one tell Gretta this."

I raised my hands. "No, nothing like that. I'm just, uh, particularly interested in hunting down some slimes. We're both new adventurers, you see."

"Ah, is just babies." She grinned and slapped me on the shoulder.

"Slimes less scary than goblins, yes? Gretta sees. Hm. Let think." Gretta rubbed at her chin. "There is . . . what is it, dripping forest? Ah, no, Sludge Forest! That is it. You go, three, maybe five miles east, down road. See sign that says, 'Danger, Keep Out.' Ignore sign. Good hunting." She nodded.

"Thank you, that sounds very helpful." I smiled. "Is there anything we can do to repay the favor?"

"You kill slimes, get levels, then you come back and buy me drink, yes?" Gretta laughed. "I be waiting for you."

I nodded.

I intended to buy her several.

We headed to the Sludge Forest.

Ken seemed somewhat less excited about the prospect than I was.

". . . So, you have an . . . actual reason to be hunting slimes?"

I grinned. "Don't worry, you'll see soon enough. Probably."

"And you can't just, uh, tell me this plan before I walk into the place filled with monsters?"

"Pfft, they're slimes. They barely count as monsters. And if I told you my plan in advance, that would limit my ability to pretend something else was my plan all along."

He laughed. "Ah, I see your logic. Very well, then." He looked cheerful, but I could see a hint of nervousness in his expression, and in the way his hand settled on the hilt of the sword at his side.

Truth be told, I was nervous, too.

HOW TO DEFEAT A DEMON KING IN TEN EASY STEPS

I didn't even have a sword. Just one of the kitchen knives I'd borrowed from Mom and a few rocks.

That would have to be enough, at least for now. My class couldn't even use swords.

(I had plans to address that problem as well, of course. There was no way I could justify taking the Hero's Sword unless I planned to wield it.)

When we reached the Sludge Forest, it looked . . . uh, pretty disgusting. Colorful goop dripped off the trees, sliding into cracks in the ground and occasionally forming pools.

Ken froze when he saw what the place actually looked like. "Could we, ah, mayhap go back to town for a bit? I think I left something behind. In my other pants. My, uh, bravery. I left my bravery in my other pants."

I patted him on the arm. "Steady, there. It's not going to be that dangerous." I paused for a moment, then added, "Probably."

Ken winced. "Look, it's not that I'm that scared of dying in the middle of nowhere in a horrifying, monster-infested wilderness. It's more that, well, that place looks rather . . . unsanitary?"

A blob of gloop fell off a nearby tree, as if to emphasize his point.

"I don't see the problem." I stared at him. "Adventuring is messy business."

"Ah, uh, yes. Certainly." He gave a little laugh. "It's just, that, well, the traditional clothing of priests and Sword Saints is, well, white. And surely you can see that this"—he waved to the forest—"would rather clash with my aesthetic?"

"Pfft. It'll be fine. We'll just stick to the roads. They don't look too bad."

The roads were only, maybe, 70 percent covered in green goop. Ken frowned.

"Don't be such a worrier!" I headed toward the path. "We'll just head in, fight a slime or two, and head back. No mess, no distress."

I liked that rhyme. I'm still proud of it.

"I . . . suppose. Very well. I shall accompany you." He straightened himself and walked to my side.

I took a better look at the area ahead of us.

I could see why this was a good place to find slime monsters: They were directly related to the goop on the trees. Given that there was a road going through this area, it probably hadn't always been like this. I suspected some kind of magical accident was involved.

Taking magic seriously and handling it responsibly is important, kids. Just ignore the fact that I started out my journey by throwing random spells at a divine artifact.

The trickiest part of the Sludge Forest was trying to identify where the goop ended and slime monster began.

I almost missed the first one we encountered. Fortunately, Ken didn't.

The slime was blue and shaped like a teardrop, about the size of a small dog. When it hopped toward us out of the goop, Ken's hand moved, drawing his sword and cutting through the air in a near-instant.

"Hyaa! Take that, foul beast!"

He missed.

Like me, Ken had an unusual class and great determination. But like me, he was still only Level 1.

HOW TO DEFEAT A DEMON KING IN TEN EASY STEPS

The slime landed between us, then hopped toward me. I jumped back, nearly slipping in a puddle of ooze.

As it neared me, I had the presence of mind to speak. "Blink."

I appeared right behind it.

The slime froze for a moment, presumably confused by the disappearance of its prey.

I jammed my knife into it from behind.

Ooze splattered on my hand, leaving mild burns. I yelped, hopping back and leaving the knife inside it.

The slime hopped, too, spinning around just in time for Ken's sword to tear it in half.

It exploded, spraying us both with goop.

> [Your party has killed a slime.
> You have gained 3 experience points.]

"Ah . . . ah," Ken stammered. His gaze gradually turned down toward his once-pristine robe. He stared for a time, as if frozen. It looked like something inside of him had fundamentally broken.

"It's okay, Ken. It's okay." I patted him. I'm pretty sure I only ended up smearing more slime on him in the process.

Ken made a whimpering sound.

"Shh. It's okay. We're going home now. We won."

He kept staring.

I paused to retrieve my knife and pick up the tiny bag of coins the monster had left behind, then grabbed his arm and gently tugged him toward the entrance of the forest.

For the first time in my life, I'd been involved in slaying a monster.

Ken looked a little better when we were finally out of the woods.

"Lesser Heal," he said, and a light washed over me. The mild burns on my hands healed immediately.

"Thanks." We split the coins and headed back to town.

We rested after we returned. Fortunately, the town had a public bath area.

Ken looked slightly less panicked after that.

We slept in town for the night.

The next day, we headed deeper into the forest.

We'd only just gotten started.

The next night, we returned to town covered in ooze once again. We split off to our respective bathing areas, washed, and met back up.

We shared a room at the inn for the night. We'd made some coin from the slimes, but it still helped to be frugal.

That night, I had a tough decision to make.

Ken and I nodded to each other.

"Level up," I said. He echoed me.

We'd each gained enough experience from hunting slimes to increase our level.

And with that, we had new options.

I could see a list of all the classes I was eligible for. Bag Mage was the first on the list, since I already was a Level 1 Bag Mage.

I had the option of using my level-up to increase my Bag Mage level from 1 to 2, or I could choose to gain Level 1 in another class I'd earned instead. That was called multi-classing, and it was relatively common for people who wanted to be flexible rather than specialized.

Taking another level in Bag Mage would have helped me work on unlocking higher-level Bag Magic—and, more importantly, Dimensional Magic. That was a tempting prospect.

I also could have taken a level in another type of magic-using class to increase my flexibility. I noted that I'd unlocked Black Mage and White Mage, which were two of the most common classes for magic use. Those were options to consider at some point.

But if I wanted to use the Hero's Sword, I needed at least one level in something that would give me access to the Sword Proficiency skill.

I had a number of class options available. Some were classic fighting classes like, well, Fighter. Others were non-fighting classes that could still gain sword proficiency, like Blacksmith, Red Mage, or Bard.

I looked through the list of everything available, smiled, and for the second time in my life, picked a class that virtually no one would ever choose.

I selected the Slime Hunter class.

The Ranger class was iconic for offering tracking skills, some alchemical skills, druidic magic, great weapon flexibility, and monster-hunting abilities.

The Monster Hunter class was a variant of Ranger, a more specialized version, losing the magic use and some other abilities in exchange for even bigger improvements to hunting specific monster types.

It was also possible to get a class variant that was even more specialized by hunting a lot of monsters of a specific type. Some of these were relatively common, like Giant Hunter, Demon Hunter, or Undead Hunter, and generally considered very useful. Dragon Hunters were among the most prestigious, offering tremendous bonuses specifically against dragons.

The Slime Hunter class was like that, but, uh, without the prestige.

They lost the monster-hunting abilities against anything other than slimes, but they were really, really good at hunting slimes.

Specifically, Slime Hunters could intuitively sense the location and direction of slimes of various different types, making tracking them a breeze. And second, they gained tremendous bonuses when fighting against slimes. Things like extra damage and bypassing a portion of the slime's defenses.

Of course, virtually no one wanted to bother being a Slime Hunter, because slimes were—for the most part—among the weakest and most common monsters available. Spending a valuable level on bonuses against slimes was, conventionally speaking, an absolutely terrible idea.

There was, however, something most adventurers knew about but didn't actually bother with—silver slimes.

Silver slimes were a type of rare slime that were notoriously difficult to kill. They were tremendously fast, and tended to run away as soon as they saw someone. Beyond that, they were also extremely resilient to damage, and virtually immune to most conventional forms of magic.

When killed, silver slimes were known to provide hundreds of times more gold and experience than normal slimes—an amount similar to high-level monsters like trolls and lesser dragons. But finding a silver slime and actually killing one was about as likely as winning a jackpot in a casino. Hunting them deliberately was generally a fool's errand, since they were both rare to find and difficult to kill even when they were encountered.

High-level adventurers could hunt silver slimes, but generally it wasn't worth their time.

So, the end result was that silver slimes were seen as a rare reason to celebrate for anyone who got lucky enough to corner one, but not something anyone should actively hope to find and hunt down.

But even with only one level in Slime Hunter, I had the ability to beat the odds.

By taking the Slime Hunter class, I'd gained several new skills.

The vast majority of them were weapon proficiencies—things like Sword Proficiency and Bow Proficiency.

To make use of those, I went and bought a simple shortsword and a short bow with the money I'd earned from slime hunting. They weren't much, but they were far superior to a kitchen knife. (Sorry, kitchen knife. You served me well, and I appreciate you.)

I bought some cheap leather armor, too. It wouldn't do much for protection, but it was better than just my traveling clothes. My Slime Hunter class had given me the necessary proficiency to wear any light or medium armor, but I couldn't afford anything better just yet.

Aside from that, I had two more interesting skills: Slime Tracking and Slime Slayer.

As soon as we got back to the Sludge Forest, I tested them out.

"Slime Tracking."

Dozens of shimmering trails appeared, overlaying my vision. They were almost blinding at first. Most of them were blue in color, with the exception of one, which was green.

"This way," I said, waving in the direction of the green trail, and began to walk.

"Understood." Ken nodded and followed me. He couldn't see the trail himself; he'd leveled up, too, but he'd taken a second level in Sword Saint instead of an absurd secondary class like mine.

It took us about a half hour to find what we were looking for—a green slime. It was largely unremarkable, save for being larger than a blue slime, poisonous, and considerably stronger.

That "poison" part was the key. That made it dangerous, even to some newly second-level adventurers.

Avoiding it would have been easy enough, but I had other ideas.

I found a nearby tree to hide behind, trying to ignore the disgusting liquid trying to seep into my boots. And from there, I took aim with my bow.

"Slime Slayer," I whispered, activating my new skill.

I fired my arrow. It hit the green slime dead-on.

The arrow pierced through the slime, leaving a splatter of goop.

Then I saw a message:

`[Slime Hunter failed to activate. Melee attack required.]`

HOW TO DEFEAT A DEMON KING IN TEN EASY STEPS

I cursed as the green slime spun around, then began rapidly hopping toward me.

"Bless." Ken stepped out in front of me, readying his sword. I fired another arrow but missed.

Ken took a swipe at the green slime, hitting it, but not hard enough to stop it. The slime crashed into him, and I heard him yelp in pain.

I cursed, dropping my bow and drawing my shortsword.

Ken fell backward, trying to push the slime off of him, but it just ended up burning his hand in the effort. He couldn't maneuver well enough to hit it while it was on top of him.

"Slime Slayer," I pronounced again, then swung the shortsword.

When my sword hit the slime, the creature burst apart in an instant.

```
[Your party has slain a Green Slime. You have earned 15
                  experience points.]
```

Ken slumped to the ground, clutching his chest.

I dropped down with him. "You okay?"

He winced. "Lesser Heal." He shuddered. "Ow. That . . . ow."

I nodded. "Sorry. I didn't realize it, but apparently that skill only works on close-range attacks."

"That's . . . kind of awful, actually. But I'm glad it worked." He pointed at the pile of treasure. "But at least we got something out of it."

"We did." I smiled. "And more than just the treasure." I pointed at the side of my head. "We just got something important."

We headed straight back to town. Even with the Lesser Heal spell, Ken was feeling sick. We suspected he'd been poisoned by contact with the slime, which wasn't something his healing spells could handle just yet. We bought an antidote, he drank it, and he slowly recovered over the course of the next few days.

We hadn't earned enough experience to level up just from killing one green slime; we'd have to kill dozens for that.

But with a better understanding of how my skills worked, we were ready for our next trip. We headed back to the forest.

"Slime Tracking."

I saw the same types of trails appear as before—blue and green. We followed one of the blue trails, discovered a blue slime, and quickly killed it. We repeated the process five more times.

The blue slimes weren't worth much experience or gold, but they were very easy to find and defeat with my new abilities. And now that I'd used Slime Tracking several times, I felt I had sufficient confirmation to have a good idea of how the skill was working.

We headed deeper into the forest. Rather than heading toward the blue and green trails, we used them to avoid running into any monsters. More trails appeared and disappeared as I moved, giving me a better idea of the skill's maximum range.

It took about two hours until I found what I was looking for: a new trail appearing in my vision. A silver one.

"Gotcha."

We headed toward the silver line. The target was easy enough to find—the brilliant steel sheen of the creature's body was a stark contrast against the bright green ooze of the forest.

I felt my heart beat faster. I'd actually found one.

A silver slime.

I pointed, then made a circling gesture with my hand. Ken nodded in understanding and moved to circle around it.

Without the tracking skill, I could have wandered for days without finding a silver slime . . . but finding it was only the first part of the problem.

Actually beating one was much, much harder.

Once Ken was in position, I raised my bow and fired.

My arrow bounced right off the creature's side.

I muttered a curse. This wasn't unexpected—silver slimes were notoriously resilient—but I'd hoped to get in a lucky shot.

The slime did exactly what I'd expected in response—it ran.

Or rather, it hopped. It hopped very, very fast.

I dropped my bow and rushed after it, but there was no chance I could catch it on my own. Fortunately, Ken was already waiting on the opposite side of the clearing.

I chased the slime right toward him.

Ken slashed the slime, and I heard a loud clang on the impact. The slime froze, leaking silvery goop from a cut in its surface.

Then, before I could get close to it or Ken could swing again, it opened its mouth and breathed fire.

I did not know it could do that.

Based on Ken's panicked expression as he fell backward, I didn't think he'd known that, either.

So, following that, we had two problems.

One, the slime was running (really hopping) away again, and two, Ken was on fire. He was on fire a lot.

"Aaah!" he screamed.

"Aaaaaaah!" I replied articulately.

Not being trained for fire safety, I simply doused him with a healing potion. That let off some kind of smoke, which might not have been healthy, but it did put out some of the fire.

After that, Ken rolled around in the green ooze on the forest floor a bit.

I reached down to help him up, but he shook his head. "After it, quick! There's still time!"

I nodded gravely. "You will be avenged."

"I'm not actually dead—"

I bolted after the slime.

I had two trails to follow now—one of dripping goop and the other a silvery line in my vision. As long as it stayed within range, I could follow it.

Unfortunately, it was faster than I was, so chasing it meant that it would eventually get out of range unless I did something to change the chase.

After following it a short way, I climbed a tree.

The slime on the trees was slippery and disgusting, but fortunately, not actually dangerous. At least as far as I knew.

I wasn't quite sure I could climb back down safely, but I had a plan for that.

From the high vantage point atop the tree, I could just barely see the slime hopping away in the distance, still looking panicked.

"Blink."

I hadn't teleported that far with Blink before, but the slime was still within line of sight. It worked.

I appeared right in front of the slime.

HOW TO DEFEAT A DEMON KING IN TEN EASY STEPS

It was briefly startled.

"Slime Slayer."

I brought my sword upward.

The silver slime fell into two perfect halves.

```
[Your party has killed a silver slime.
 You have earned 1,723 experience points.]
```

For the first time since the start of my plans, one of my crazy ideas had actually worked.

STEP FIVE

DEFEAT THE DEADLY MONSTERS TO INCREASE YOUR ABILITIES

KEN, WHO DEFINITELY WASN'T dead but still had been thoroughly avenged, was looking much better by the time I got back to him. He'd healed his own injuries with his magic.

He was, like me, covered in goop. But his smile and thumbs-up gesture showed that he, too, had received an absurd number of experience points.

I handed him half the impressive pile of silver coins the silver slime had dropped when it died, then we headed back to town.

I intended to shower forever.

We rented a room at a fancy inn. One with showers. Beautiful, amazing showers.

I felt a little sorry for the staff of the inn that would have to clean up after us. I tipped heavily.

When I closed my eyes in the shower, I saw three beautiful, amazing messages.

    [You have gained a level. You have reached level 3.]
    [You have gained a level. You have reached level 4.]
    [You have gained a level. You have reached level 5.]

The silver slime had given us months' worth of experience and coins in a single fight.

At that point, I had another critical decision to make.

Every time I gained a level, I could choose which class to allocate that level to. Higher levels in a specific class would unlock more powerful abilities geared toward that class. In addition, each level in a class also improved a person's physical (and sometimes magical) abilities. For example, levels in a Blacksmith class would permanently increase someone's physical strength, and levels in any magic-using class would provide an increased amount of mana available for casting spells.

Many of the most powerful skills and spells required a high level in one specific class, so spreading levels out all over the place wasn't generally considered wise. If I wanted to excel in any given field, I'd eventually have to choose something to specialize in.

So did I want to invest more in my Slime Hunter class to make hunting slimes even more efficient? While I didn't see myself hunting slimes forever, levels in this class would also improve my general physical combat abilities, so it was a viable option.

Did I want to level my Bag Mage class instead, and hope I could unlock more powerful Dimensional Magic? This was a gamble, since I didn't know what kind of Dimensional Magic was available to a high-level Bag Mage, but I would also be increasing my available mana each time I gained a level.

Or did I want to choose a third class entirely, perhaps a more conventional one? If I wanted to fight the Demon King directly at some point in time, taking a class designed for combat—like a Fighter or Fire Mage class—might be a wise choice.

It was a difficult decision, but for my long-term plans, Dimensional Magic was essential.

There were two main reasons for this.

HOW TO DEFEAT A DEMON KING IN TEN EASY STEPS

First, when I'd last attempted to store the pedestal that held the Hero's Sword in my Inventory, the message in response was that the pedestal had resisted my spell. Magic resistance was something that could, in theory, be overridden by powerful-enough magic—and that meant a higher level in the relevant class, a higher skill level, or a more powerful individual spell.

Second, Dimensional Magic was extraordinarily rare, and something that I didn't think the Demon King was likely to have developed complete countermeasures against. I had no illusions about beating the Demon King in a sword fight, even with the Hero's Sword; I'd need every advantage I could get, and Dimensional Magic felt like one of the best possible ways to get the edge I needed.

So I leveled up my Bag Mage class three times.

I immediately felt amazing.

There was a brief euphoric feeling as I sensed new power and a wider well of mana flowing within me. And, despite choosing a magic-wielding class, I felt just a little bit tougher, too. I'd felt some improvement when I'd gained my first level, but this was much more obvious; gaining three levels at once was a tremendous increase in my capabilities.

Beyond those benefits, I'd also acquired something entirely new.

[You have learned a new skill: Cheapskate.]

I stared at the skill, uncertain.

What the heck was that? Something that gave me discounts on buying things . . . ? No, that didn't make sense. That would require some kind of mind control.

Maybe . . .

I tried casting Blink. Casting it once didn't feel any different, but after casting it three times, I didn't feel like I'd reached my limit. I cast it again and again, my grin widening with each successful use. I didn't stop until after I'd cast the spell a total of eight times.

Cheapskate, it seemed, didn't save me money—it saved me mana.

Sadly, I couldn't tell exactly how much Cheapskate was saving, since increasing my level had also increased my available mana. Either way, gaining the levels had made a huge improvement to how may spells I could cast in a row. For an ordinary Bag Mage, that savings might have simply been a convenience. For me, it was a lifesaver.

Fully showered and leveled up, I indulged myself in ordering food delivered to the room, then had a fitful sleep for the night.

Two months passed.

Many, many silver slimes were killed.

Ken and I hunted each day. Most days, we only managed to find a single slime. Sometimes, if we were lucky, we'd find two or three.

The plan was working masterfully; we were earning experience and gold at a rate comparable to high-level adventurers but with virtually no risk.

We eventually stopped for three main reasons.

One, I was concerned about overhunting the region. Monsters respawned over time, but their reproductive process was poorly understood. If I killed too many silver slimes, I was worried I'd wipe them out entirely from the area and ruin the prospect of others—or even ourselves—doing the same thing again in the future.

The second problem was diminishing returns. While we did earn significant experience for killing the slimes, as we gained higher and higher levels, the increasing experience requirements meant that killing slimes became progressively less efficient.

Toward the end, it was taking us several days of killing one or two slimes a day to earn a single level. And while that is actually pretty impressive by ordinary leveling standards, we'd gotten used to it being super easy at the start, so we didn't have the kind of patience for it that we should have.

And third, it was very, very boring.

While storing a rock (or a ring, or whatever) over and over was more boring in concept, that was something I could do casually while in the midst of other activities. This dominated nearly our entire day, and it was exhausting, smelly work.

I have no complaints about the results, but it's not something I would ever want to repeat.

After all that hunting, we'd gained several levels. We were both a total of Level 11. In my case, that meant nine levels of Bag Mage and two levels of Slime Hunter.

That extra Slime Hunter level didn't get me much, just a skill called Ambidexterity. It felt a little weird being able to use my off hand almost as well as my main hand, but I wasn't going to complain about it. I did wonder what would happen if someone who was naturally ambidextrous got the skill, though. Would they get better with using both hands? Skills were often a mystery like that.

More importantly, being Level 9 as a Bag Mage got me a few new skills, as well as several new spells.

Skill-wise, the first thing I got was something called Unencumbered. That made it easier for me to wear or carry items without feeling their weight, even if they weren't in my Inventory. The amount I could carry without feeling it would depend on my level in the skill. I was pleased, since it seemed like the kind of thing I could increase just by... wearing stuff.

Beyond that, I got two more items of interest. One was Double Bag, which let me have two separate inventories, each with the same capacity. This didn't seem super immediately useful, especially since I could already carry an incredible number of items, but I figured it would come in handy at some point. Maybe I could use it for easier organization, or just fill up my second bag with something I didn't want to contaminate the things in the first, like anything poisonous.

(I wasn't actually sure if items inside the Inventory interacted with each other. That was worth testing at some point. Preferably without making my Inventory explode by putting two volatile things next to each other.)

Finally, my most important new skill was Carry Anything.

It enabled me to safely carry items that would normally hurt anyone who didn't meet certain requirements. It didn't actually let me use those items, but it meant that I could pick up a cursed item and put it back down without hurting myself. That was neat.

Did it let me pull a certain legendary sword out of a certain stone in a shrine?

Of course not. There was no way it would be that simple. I

grumbled a little bit after my last failed attempt, but it wasn't exactly unexpected.

"Maybe I should try taking a level in Thief..." I mumbled.

"People have already tried to use the Pickpocket skill on the sword. Repeatedly," Ken explained. "It's a clever notion, but apparently even high-level Thieves have difficulty stealing things that are embedded in an enchanted platform."

I sighed. "I suppose Thief might still be useful anyway. Could I steal things directly into my Inventory? Maybe I could use that to disarm people..."

"I don't think taking levels in Thief is going to be good for your heroic reputation."

I shrugged. "I don't really care about that. I care about succeeding. If I have to take some sketchy classes to accomplish that, I'll do it. But I'll hold off on Thief for the moment. I still think I can get more useful stuff out of higher-level magic."

I'd already gotten some pretty neat spells just by increasing my Bag Mage level to nine.

Spells were a little strange. In order to learn a new spell, you'd have to have both the required level in the skill—like say, level 25 in Dimensional Magic—and a high-enough level in the appropriate class. So you could either get a spell when you reached a specific skill threshold (if your class level was already high enough), or right when you leveled up (if your skill level was already high enough).

There were also some weird rare spells that weren't learned automatically, but that you could learn from books or scrolls if you met the appropriate requirements.

Anyway, in my case, I got most of my new spells upon leveling, since I used my skills so much more than normal people in my level range.

In terms of Bag Magic, I learned three new spells—View, Sort, and Project.

View projected a list of all the current items in my Inventory into a glowing phantasmal parchment in front of me. I could already see my own Inventory without it, but this projection was visible to other people. That meant it would be useful for people like shopkeepers, I assumed.

Sort could be used to change the order of how those items were listed—like by category or date obtained.

And Project created a solid illusion of one of the items from my list so that I could show it to someone. The illusion could be picked up and moved around, but it wasn't very durable and didn't have any of the properties of the original item. The spell was designed for displaying merchandise, not for fighting.

They were all potentially useful, but Project excited me the most. It would be especially helpful if I actually got up to any thievery, since I could project a duplicate of whatever I took. A quick test told me that the illusions were pretty hard to tell apart at a glance, and they lasted quite a while.

Most important, though, were my new Dimensional Magic spells.

The Phase spell let me move through walls and other solid objects. (No, it didn't let me Phase my hand through the pedestal beneath the sword to try to steal it that way. I did try. My hand bounced off an invisible shield.)

And Anchor would temporarily make a target immune to

teleportation. Useful if I ran into any monsters or traps that wanted to move me around.

In Ken's case, he was now a Level 9 Sword Saint... and a Level 2 Fashionista.

He'd unlocked a number of new spells throughout the leveling process, most importantly Moderate Heal, Antidote, Protect, and Bless Weapon. Those spells did exactly what they sounded like.

I didn't know what the Fashionista levels were for. He told me he had "big plans" and that it would be a surprise.

I tried not to be too nervous about that—I was too busy being worried about something far more important.

It was time to go to our first dungeon.

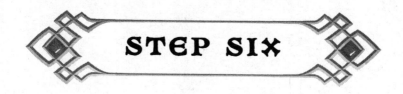

STEP SIX

USE THE TRADITIONAL STEPS TO DEFEAT EACH DUNGEON

IT TOOK CLOSE TO a week to get to our destination—a colossal withered tree. Once, it might have stood hundreds of feet in height. Now, it was merely about fifty, with the entire top portion having been burned away. Even centuries after the event, I could see hints of ashes mixed in with the nearby dirt and stone.

According to legend, it was once one of the five Sacred Silver Trees that had assisted one of the first Heroes with their journey. In the aftermath of the failure of the Water Temple Hero—the Hero who disappeared into the Water Temple without ever returning—the Demon King had taken it upon himself to obliterate many of the Hero's traditional allies.

Nearly all the Sacred Silver Trees had been among them.

Now it had three holes in the base that looked almost like eyes and a mouth, stretched out in one final scream. It was a harrowing sight.

I steeled myself. This was no longer simply a remnant of the past or the corpse of an ancient being; it was the entrance to a labyrinth—the Wood Temple, the first of the Five Temples.

Each of the Five Temples was dedicated to a single element. That theme would influence both the entrance and, at times, the contents of the temple itself.

The temples served a critical function. They each held a single piece of the Pentacrest, a legendary artifact that, once assembled, would give the holder the power to breach the barrier around the

Demon King's fortress. Without it, confronting the Demon King was largely impossible.

Earning one piece would be the first step toward a true path to victory.

Ken and I walked to the side of the tree. I put a hand on the tree's bark. "I'm sorry that it ended for you like this. You'll be avenged."

With that, I led the way into the tree's gaping maw.

"Are you really sure this is such a good idea?" Ken sounded nervous as I led the way inside. I had a sword in one hand and a lantern in the other as I led the way down the stairway inside the tree's mouth.

I don't know why there was a stairway in the tree's mouth. Probably the same reason there are weird "dungeons" that refill themselves with loot every hundred years—the gods have some odd ways of looking at how Heroes should prove their worth.

"No, of course I'm not sure it's a good idea. I am sure, however, that it's something I want to do. Something I need to do. This world needs saving, Ken."

"It does . . . it's just . . . we don't have all the things a Hero would normally have for a journey like this. We don't have a faerie guide, any musical instruments, bombs . . ."

"I don't think we're going to need explosives to make our way through a tree, Ken. Even if it's a monster-infested tree that has . . ."—I frowned as I reached the bottom of the stairs—". . . a weirdly elaborate stone building beneath it."

I'd heard legends about the Five Temples before, of course. I'd studied them extensively. But there was still something strange about walking from a forest into a tree and finding what looked like an ancient palace inside.

The first room was almost perfectly square, about twenty feet in each direction, with solid gray stone floors and walls.

It was lit by ever-burning magical torches. I put a hand on one of them, impressed. "Inventory."

```
[Your Bag Magic has successfully overcome this object's
                   Magic Resistance.]
```

A smirk crossed my face as the magic torch vanished into my Inventory. Apparently, my Bag Mage level and Inventory skill level were high enough to overcome some magic resistance now. If I kept working at it, maybe I'd eventually be able to grab some more secure items.

The room dimmed, but there were still three other torches, so I thought it was probably fine.

"That actually worked?" Ken's expression showed a mixture of surprise and concern. I suppose he probably wasn't thrilled that I was taking something that could qualify as a sacred object.

"Yeah, I'm surprised it worked, too. I figured I'd need that Pickpocket skill or something to get it off the wall, but no, apparently the enchantments here aren't as secure as the sword's."

"Are you just going to steal everything in here?"

I shrugged. "I mean, not everything. Some things won't be useful."

Ken groaned. "Let's get this over with."

Aside from the torches, the room was mostly unadorned. There were a couple of conspicuous large stone blocks toward the center, as well as three doors—one straight ahead from the stairs, one on the left side of the room, and one on the right.

All the doors were stone, rather than wood. They had creases in the center and gems located on the right side. It was a bit of an odd design, but I'd heard about it before—if we touched the gem after meeting whatever the requirements were, the door would open for us.

The one straight ahead of us had a huge lock on it, as well as a comically large lock painted on it.

"I think it might be locked, Ken."

"I think you might be right."

The other two doors didn't have any such symbols. I presumed they were either unlocked or opened by a mechanism connected to the big stone blocks in the center.

"Now's probably the time to get ready," I instructed Ken.

He nodded, casting a suite of beneficial spells on us. "Protect. Bless. Bless Weapon. Lesser Strength." He took a breath after that. Using that much mana rapidly was a bit draining, but as long as this room was safe, we could always rest back here if we needed to. And I vastly preferred being overprepared rather than under.

We went left first, swords drawn and ready.

Imposing stone pillars were interspersed throughout the chamber, running from floor to ceiling. Beyond that, I didn't see anything notable at first. There were no other doors, no obvious monsters, no clear pressure plates to indicate traps or puzzles.

I frowned, stepping inside.

I'd made a novice mistake. I'd looked down and ahead, but I'd forgotten to look up.

HOW TO DEFEAT A DEMON KING IN TEN EASY STEPS

There was a horrifying screech as the room's threats descended from the ceiling, fangs wide and ready to rend flesh from bone.

The first of the creatures attacked before I could properly react, trying to take a bite out of my shoulder. I felt a surge of panic as it closed its jaws... and completely failed to pierce my ordinary leather armor.

I slapped the bat off my shoulder, blinking. "Is... that an ordinary fruit bat?"

"I'm certain it must not be. Surely it is some sort of fearsome bat demon!"

I narrowed my eyes. "Pretty sure that's a fruit bat."

Another bat slammed into me, headfirst. I ignored it. It couldn't have weighed more than a couple pounds.

Ken took a swing at it while it retreated, but missed.

"Are we actually fighting these?" I gestured with my lantern. "I feel kind of bad about it. They just live here."

Another bat flew at Ken, but he stepped out of the way. It crashed into a wall.

"They also don't seem very smart."

Ken nodded. "They are but the weakest of the Demon King's minions. A mere taste of his formidable power."

"Right, right." I frowned. "I just feel sort of bad for them. Can we check the other room?"

"Sure, I guess." Ken dodged another bat, and we stepped out of the room.

The bats didn't follow us, in spite of the door being wide open. "Weird. How do you think they eat down here? I didn't see any food."

"They're demons, Yui. They don't need to eat."

I was still pretty sure they were just fruit bats, but I shrugged a shoulder. "Okay, sure. Other door?"

"Other door."

We headed to the other door, swinging it open to find a similar room—but one with threats that even I wouldn't balk at fighting.

Five human skeletons faced us, each holding a pair of wicked-looking curved blades. They stared at us with glowing red motes of light in their otherwise empty eye sockets, but remained motionless as we stood in the doorway.

I'll admit it—I was a little intimidated. Human skeletons were a lot scarier than slimes and fruit bats. I did have some questions about how they were going to move, or even how they were standing without any muscles, but I didn't bother saying them out loud.

Instead, I focused on the fact that they hadn't stepped out of their room.

"Ken, why are they just standing there? I don't remember reading about anything like that."

"Ah, it's one of the ancient blessings of the Silver Goddesses. It prevents monsters from moving between the rooms of a dungeon."

I blinked. "So . . . they're just going to stand there, harmlessly staring at us unless we go inside?"

"Yes. No monster of their level could possibly resist the powers of the goddesses."

"Huh." I sheathed my sword, taking out my bow. "Okay, then."

"What are you—?"

I shot one of the skeletons in the face.

Or at least, I tried to.

My arrow disappeared the moment it went into the doorway. "What?"

"Ah, yes, the same blessings of the Silver Goddesses unfortunately prevent projectiles from going between rooms."

I sighed. "Okay. Do you have any anti-undead spells?"

Ken looked slightly abashed. "A traditional priest would, but as a Sword Saint..." He shook his head. "My Bless Weapon spell should allow our ordinary swords to work against them, however."

I nodded at that. "Okay. Let's do this thing."

I switched back to my sword. Then, I set down my lantern and retrieved the magic torch from my Inventory. It seemed pretty sturdy, and I figured I could use it as an off-hand weapon.

With that, we stepped inside.

The skeletons began moving immediately. Some toward us, some... not. I was worried at first they were moving into flanking positions, but honestly, I couldn't see any logic to their movements.

The room was about forty feet across, so it gave us plenty of room to maneuver. Ken and I stayed close. As the first skeleton neared us, Ken lashed out immediately, batting one of its swords out of the way.

I took the opening, using my torch to deflect the skeleton's other sword and landing a slice across the skeleton's rib cage. Bones splintered, but the skeleton remained animated, pulling back and swiping at us.

Ken and I danced backward, avoiding both of its slices. A second skeleton came at Ken from the right, and he managed a downward chop that cut off one of its legs before it got too close. It hit the floor, then just sort of started swinging harmlessly at the air.

I focused on the first skeleton, dodging another pair of rhythmic sweeps from its blades and then smashing it in the face with my torch. It staggered back, thrashing wildly and missing me entirely.

I lunged in, jabbing my sword under its chin. The sword pierced upward with a crack, and the lights in its eyes faded.

[Your party has killed a skeleton.
You have earned 70 experience points.]

I took a moment to boggle at the idea of "killing" a skeleton, then ducked a swing from one of the other skeletons that had drawn near.

Two of the others had wandered into a corner, and they were flailing wildly. I had no idea why.

Ken deftly hopped past the swipes of the floor-bound skeleton, then brought his sword down on its neck, cutting straight through with ease.

[Your party has killed a skeleton.
You have earned 70 experience points.]

I parried two strikes from the newest approaching skeleton without any difficulty. It was about as fast as I was, but it always swung both swords at the same time, rather than using them in a coordinated fashion. It also seemed to favor simple, direct movements—straight up and down or straight across. They were heavily telegraphed and easy to dodge or parry once I'd recognized the sequence.

I took a few more moments to make certain I had the pattern down, then made a simple movement as it withdrew from an attack, cutting a skeletal hand off at the wrist.

Then, as it repeated its motions for the next attack, I did the same. Two fleshless hands clattered to the ground, each carrying a rusty blade.

It kept swinging anyway but didn't even adjust its distance. It just... sort of swung at the air, as if it still had hands.

I briefly felt sorry for it, but this was a skeleton, not a harmless fruit bat. Another flick of my blade took off its head.

```
[Your party has killed a skeleton.
 You have earned 70 experience points.]
```

We closed in on the last two skeletons. It was only at that point that I realized that one of them had a golden key hidden in its rib cage. That was a little weird, but it seemed like a poor time to question it, so I focused on the fighting.

A few moments later, the battle was over. We knew the pattern to fighting the skeletons now, and they were largely harmless in small numbers.

The golden key clattered to the ground as the last of the skeletons fell. Upon close inspection, it was comically large. I presumed it corresponded to the equally silly lock on the previous room's door.

I poked it with my sword once or twice, just to make sure it wasn't a mimic or something. I'd heard of those things, and I wasn't going to let one bite me. Not even once.

When the key remained still, I gave it a dubious glower, then carefully picked it up.

"Well fought." Ken slapped me on the shoulder. "We might make it through this place after all."

I nodded. "See anything else of value in here?"

He made a gesture at one of the nearby walls. "I believe I've uncovered a secret door."

I approached the wall he'd mentioned. It was covered in huge cracks. "That's... huh. Looks more like weather damage to me."

"Were this an ordinary building, I would agree. But this is a place sacred to the Silver Goddesses. No mere weather would cause the walls harm. No, this is deliberate."

"Deliberate... cracks in the wall? Why?"

"According to the legends of the Hero, I believe this is where we are supposed to place a bomb."

I stared dubiously at the cracks. "A bomb."

"Yes."

I sighed. "The goddesses want us to blow up their domain with explosives."

Ken sighed, looking at me like I was a child. "No, Yui. It is well-known to the goddesses that the Hero favors the use of bombs. It is among his most common tools. And thus, to prepare the way for the Hero, they hide secret treasures for him in passages accessible by such devices."

"Okay. Let's think about that for a minute. These places are all supposed to be holy sites, which the goddesses know will eventually be taken over by demons, right?"

"Yes. In each cycle, the Demon King takes these sacred places and corrupts them, seeking to draw in their power for his own wicked purposes. He then hides the keys to his own lair within them, knowing that the power of his foul minions will make it so that none other than the Hero can reach them."

"I... okay. Let's say you're one of the Silver Goddesses."

"That seems a little sacrilegious, but I understand the hypothetical. Go on."

"You want to put in treasures that only the Hero can reach."

"Right."

"Other people can make bombs."

"Well, hypothetically—"

"Even demons."

He nodded. "True, though most wouldn't."

"And you have enchantments that can make it so that only a Hero can access something. Like, you know, the one on the pedestal for the Hero's Sword."

Ken folded his arms. "I see where you're going with that, but consider that if the goddesses put in a bunch of rooms that were warded by such potent enchantments, the Demon King could easily identify those rooms. Perhaps he could find a way to bypass them and get the treasure inside!"

"I mean, you figured out the cracks in the wall at a glance. Couldn't he just see those and, you know, put down a bomb? Or, like, hit it really hard? He's a Demon King."

"I . . . well, that wouldn't be traditional . . ."

"Okay, Ken. Never mind. Let's just get this over with and find out what's inside."

Ken breathed a sigh of relief. "Good, good. These discussions worry me at times, Yui. I understand you have concerns, but they border on heretical."

"Sorry. I'll try to be a little more, uh, sensitive. Okay. Let's get in there."

"We don't have any bombs. How would we—?"

I rolled my eyes. "Phase."

I stuck my arm through the wall.

"That's... I think that's cheating."

I shrugged. "If it works, it works. Come on, I'll cast it on you as well."

"I... don't think... maybe I'll just wait here?"

I sighed. "Okay."

I stepped through the wall, sword at the ready. My Phase spell let me pass through walls, but I didn't think it would make me incorporeal to other things, like monster attacks. That was a little strange, too, but magic often seemed arbitrary to me.

There were no monsters in this room—just a single large, ornate box. There were no other doors in the room, either. Ken had been right about the goddesses hiding treasure, I guess.

I approached the box cautiously.

Could be a mimic.

I hit the box repeatedly. Nothing happened.

I waited a few seconds, then flipped the latch and opened it.

Inside the box was a small circular device with a needle pointed to the upper-right side. It took me a minute to realize what I was seeing.

A compass.

I picked it up, quickly noticing that it didn't have a "north" symbol on the top. I walked over to the wall, recast Phase, and walked back out to show the object to Ken.

"A compass! That will show us the way to the end of the dungeon, where we will face a terrible boss monster."

"Hm." I considered that for a moment.

"I . . . don't like it when you get that look, Yui."

I checked the compass. "Give me a minute."

I Phased back into the room, feeling grateful for the Cheapskate skill's reduction to my mana costs. I barely felt winded from the effort.

I found the wall nearest to where the compass was pointing, then cast Phase again.

There was nothing saying I could only Phase through cracked walls, after all.

I quickly found myself inside solid rock. Simply walking through walls wouldn't always lead me into another room, of course—I must have found a place that was on the outer boundaries of the dungeon. I was still incorporeal, though, and I could keep moving if I wanted to.

I moved forward a few steps, then turned back. I could have gone farther, but I was worried about what might happen if the spell wore off while I was still inside solid stone. I imagined it wouldn't end well for me.

Then, I went back to Ken. "I think I could probably get us all the way through to the boss room with Phase, as long as it isn't higher or lower than we are."

"Yui. Please. I beg you. No shortcuts, unless they are those the goddess wills us to take."

"Look, Ken, I'm not going to agree to that as a general rule, but if it's important to you, we can scout a few more of the rooms first."

"Thank you. Thank you." Ken sounded immensely grateful. "Can we go back and just try the key in the first room?"

"Sure."

I did wonder why the Demon King would have left a key to get farther into this place inside one of his skeletons, but I felt that asking any more probing questions was likely to cause Ken to have some sort of breakdown, so I kept it to myself.

We went back to the first room. As expected, the key went easily into the lock. When we turned the key, the door slid open.

Inside the next room were three more skeletons. We stepped in and dispatched them with ease. There was an open doorway on the other side, so we stepped through it.

Inside the next room we found a handful of slimes, a single large block, and two doorways. The doorway on the left had a strange, glowing magical seal on it. The doorway on the right was open.

"Slime Slayer." I stepped in, easily dispatching the slimes with a single cut each.

"Hm." Ken glanced at the large block and the sealed door. "A puzzle room. Truly, this place is a testament to the magnificence of the goddesses. If one was a true Hero, they could seek to solve this puzzle and gain access to the ancient secrets of the hidden chamber, but alas, I..."

I walked over to the block, then shoved it. It slid to the left. There was a melodic sound, then the seal on the left door opened.

Ken stared at me in wide-eyed shock. "Yui...how did you...?"

"It's a block, Ken. There are really only so many things you can do with it."

"But...how did you know which way it was supposed to go?"

"I didn't. If it didn't go left, I would have just shoved it in another direction."

Ken stared at me for another moment, then nodded slowly. "Yes... it makes sense. Trial and error. Such is a common method the Hero uses to resolve such problems."

"Are we checking the sealed room?"

He nodded. "I believe that would be wise. At times, the goddess leaves more treasures or hints for the Hero in such rooms."

I led the way inside. I was a little startled by what it contained.

The floor of the room was pitch black, as if it stood upon the emptiness of the void between the stars.

Two fires burned on the left and right sides, seemingly without origin.

In the center stood a bearded old man. "So. You have finally come..." he said, then broke into a cough.

"Are... you okay?" I stepped in, sheathing my sword.

He coughed again, then looked up at me, squinting. "Yes... it has simply been so long..."

"Inventory. Remove flask." A flask of water appeared in my hand, and I offered it to the old man. "Here, drink."

He accepted the flask, drinking. "Thank you, Hero..." He frowned, looking me over. "You... wait. You look a little... different from what I was expecting."

"Let's not worry about little details. Uh, so, what are you doing here?"

"Ah, yes, forgive me." He handed the water flask back to me, and I returned it to my Inventory. "Long have I awaited the coming of the Hero, in order to give him an ancient secret."

Ooh, I thought. *I like ancient secrets.*

"And that secret would be?"

The old man cleared his throat, standing up a little straighter. "Behold: The westmost peninsula hides a great secret."

I blinked. "O...kay? What sort of secret?"

The old man shrugged. "I have no idea."

"Westmost in terms of this particular kingdom, or...?"

"That is not for me to know, Hero. You must take the wisdom of the goddesses and use it on your own. Were you not taught these things?"

"I, uh, was just testing you?"

He nodded gravely. "Yes, of course...testing is the way of the goddesses. You go with their blessing indeed."

I wiped my forehead. Was I sweating? Maybe a little. "Right. Do you want us to get you out of here, maybe?"

He shook his head sadly. "It is kind of you to offer, Hero. But alas, my responsibility is not yet done. I must now await the coming of the next Hero."

"...What, really? Like, more than a hundred years?"

He frowned. "More? Shouldn't it be exactly...?"

I put up my hands defensively. "I, uh, got here really fast. Extra Fast Hero, that's me. Most Heroes are slower, so, uh, little over a hundred years."

"Oh!" The old man smiled. "You must be similar to the Speedy Runner Hero. He was a strange one. Only walked in here for a moment, then walked back out backward, firing an arrow with a bomb strapped to it. I never understood why."

"That...sounds horrible. Were you hurt?"

"Oh, no. I'm quite difficult to harm, I assure you. I'm immortal and virtually invincible."

I coughed. "In... vincible? Could you... maybe come fight the Demon King, then? I'm sure a bit of fresh air would be nice."

"Sadly, my immortality is contingent on me remaining here. And if I were to leave, future Heroes would not learn this very important, definitely necessary secret."

I didn't know what to say to that. I just... kind of stood there for a minute. "Do you, like, want a book or something? I think I have a couple."

"Oh, please. Anything. You have no idea how boring this place is."

"Right. Inventory."

I searched through the gleaming symbols in my view for books, pressing them one at a time. I handed him every book I had, then resolved to come back with more later. "You, uh, take care of yourself."

"You as well, Hero. Goddess be with you."

I left that room feeling very sincerely disturbed.

"That was kind of you," Ken said. "I don't think most Heroes would worry so much about the fate of a single old man."

There was something deeply wrong with that, too, if Ken was right.

The more I considered the nature of the dungeons and the cycle of the Hero and the Demon King, the more I was disturbed.

I stepped into the next open door with renewed determination. The skeletons within fell easily to Ken's sword and my own.

We paused briefly for Ken to renew our Bless Weapon spells. There were two more doors in this room, one straight across and one to our left. We chose the left door.

Inside were three strange, green-skinned humanoid creatures.

They screeched loudly as we entered, drawing knives from their belts.

"Uh, hello," I raised my hands. "Can we ta—"

One of them hurled a knife at me. Ken stepped in, his blade moving in a flash to deflect the knife. "Goblins. You can't reason with them."

I tightened my jaw but braced myself. If I spoke their language, maybe... but I didn't.

They rushed forward, knives in hand. I couldn't lose my resolve.

The goblins were a bit shorter than we were, maybe four and a half feet in height. Consequently, they also had shorter limbs. Between that and their shorter weapons, well, they'd made a pretty big mistake by charging in close.

Reach is a huge advantage in a fight. Even with a shortsword, with my longer limbs, I had nearly two feet in extra reach. Ken, taller than me and with a longer weapon, had even more.

The goblins never got close.

[Your party has killed a goblin. You have earned 150 experience points.]

I frowned as they vanished upon their death, leaving behind little more than dust. Why did that happen with some monsters?

One of them did leave something behind, though. Not a body—a piece of wood.

I frowned, stabbed it a couple times to check if it was a mimic, and then picked it up.

Ken gasped. "The boomerang! The legendary boomerang, one of the iconic weapons of the Hero!"

I blinked. "I'm... pretty sure this is just a normal boomerang, Ken."

"Of course. We wouldn't find the magic boomerang so early in our quest, Yui. But finding the boomerang is an important step! It is a potent weapon against flying creatures."

I narrowed my eyes. "It's... pretty much just a piece of wood. Wouldn't arrows be more effective?"

"Ah, in terms of sheer damage, yes. But the boomerang, when hurled by the Hero, will return unerringly! It can be used an unlimited amount of times. And with sufficient skill, it can even be used to retrieve distant objects!"

I squinted at the boomerang some more, unimpressed. "You want it, then?"

"I couldn't possibly..." Ken hesitated. "I'm no Hero, Yui."

"Neither am I, if we're counting purely by classes. Come on. You clearly want it."

I extended a hand to him.

"I..." He reached out gingerly, like it was going to bite him.

I pressed the boomerang into his hands. "See? It's fine, Ken. It's yours now."

"I... thank you, Yui. I don't know what to say." He stood a little straighter then. "I will endeavor to prove worthy of this great honor."

I nodded. "I'm sure you'll do fine. Come on."

That path went on a little farther. We fought a few more skeletons and slimes, but nothing proved dangerous.

One of the slimes dropped something when it vanished—a crude map. It had virtually no information, just a bunch of squares to represent rooms.

One of the rooms was flashing red, though.

After a moment of orienting ourselves, we identified the entrance, and I realized that the flashing room corresponded to the same direction the compass was facing.

The boss room, then. We knew the route to the end of the dungeon.

We didn't go that way first, though. Ken insisted that exploring the dungeon for more equipment was of the utmost importance if we wished to survive our entire journey. So we continued on a path that would lead us away from the boss room, at least for the moment.

More skeletons fell easily to our blades.

After a couple more rooms, we found our first trapped room.

There were four blocks in the corners of the room, each covered in wicked spikes. They had eyelike symbols on each of their sides. The blocks were as tall as I was and probably about four feet wide, with the spikes adding a couple extra feet of danger to each of them. Fortunately, we could see them from the doorway.

In the center of the room were several other blocks in a strange formation, clearly surrounding something. These didn't have spikes on them; they simply served as a barricade.

Given that the spiked blocks were in corners that weren't anywhere close to the center, and there were no monsters present, I figured something was going to make the spiked blocks move.

"Any ideas, Ken?"

"I believe I know this one. When you step inside, those blocks will rapidly converge. If you are not hasty enough, you will be impaled on the spikes."

I nodded. "So, it's more of a dexterity and speed challenge?"

"Yes. And proper timing. The spiked blocks will withdraw a few moments after you trigger them. You can lure them out, then rush forward as they withdraw."

I tested that quickly by stepping forward, then back.

True to Ken's word, the spiked blocks shot forward as soon as I stepped in. They moved in a straight line, meeting just in front of the doorway without colliding with each other. If I hadn't stepped back, I would have been jabbed with those wicked spikes within a few moments.

Then, slowly, they floated back toward their original positions. That took about twice as long as it had taken for them to rush inward.

I tossed a rock onto the floor. The traps didn't react.

Hmm.

"Could we jump through, or do they sense any sort of movement that people make?"

Ken shrugged. "I don't know how they work, sorry."

I nodded slowly. "Okay. Easy enough."

I stepped in, luring the spiked blocks out, then rushed forward with Ken as the blocks retracted. We found a spot next to the large blocks in the center, out of a direct line from the spiked blocks.

I worried the spiked blocks might rush at us again, but they didn't. "They only move in one direction?"

"No, but they can only move orthogonally from their starting position, like tower game pieces. And they only move if you walk in front of the eyes on one of the sides. As long as we stand at a diagonal from them, they won't move."

"Hmm. That means..."

I cautiously walked closer to one of the blocks. If it could only move orthogonally, and only if the eyes saw me...

I reached out and touched one of the spikes from an angle. The block didn't move.

A grin stretched across my face.

"Inventory."

And, with a thought, the block slipped inside.

Ken stared at me. "You..."

I turned back to him. "Do these only respond to human movement, or any movement?"

"I don't know."

I smirked. "We'll find out soon."

A few minutes later, I had three more spiked blocks in my Inventory.

Then, we simply had to deal with the stone blocks in the center of the room.

I shoved on the first one. It didn't budge.

A few more shoves, though, and one of them slipped out of the way to reveal a stairway.

We walked down cautiously.

It was darker below, and I kept a torch in hand as we descended.

More bats flew at us. I rolled my eyes. "Shoo." I swatted them out of the way as they approached.

Toward the end of the passage, we found our reward.

It was, to all appearances, a simple wooden bow.

"Amazing!" Ken reached out toward it, then pulled his hand back. "You want that, too?"

HOW TO DEFEAT A DEMON KING IN TEN EASY STEPS

"I couldn't possibly..."

"I already have a bow, Ken. Go ahead."

With the utmost reverence, Ken took the bow and slipped it over his shoulders.

Then, with that in hand, we retreated back to the last room where we'd seen another door we hadn't explored.

It looked empty, aside from a bunch of stone blocks. A ton of stone blocks.

There was another door on the north side of it, wide open.

It felt like a trap.

"Ideas?" I asked Ken.

"Well, it's possible there's another secret passage. We could push on the blocks?"

I nodded in agreement. We stepped inside.

A gigantic disembodied hand, nearly as large as my entire body, floated straight out of the wall next to me. Its fingers splayed wide, then began to close as it flew toward me. I responded with a mighty battle cry, to the tune of, "Aaaaah, why are there wall hands?!"

Truly, my perfect composure under even the most surprising of situations is my most heroic quality.

Ken rushed forward, jamming his sword into the hand. It sank in deep, but the hand simply floated forward and batted him out of the way. Ken hit one of the stone blocks hard, falling to the ground.

I smashed the hand with my torch. The flames blackened a patch of its strange blue skin, but the hand opened wide again, then shot forward with great speed and tried to grapple me.

I hurled myself to the side, then jabbed the back of the hand with my shortsword.

It spun around to face me.

"Look out!" Ken cried.

Something slammed into my back, hard.

A second hand had appeared right behind me, then punched me in the back.

I winced at the sudden pain of the blow. The hand had hit me hard, nearly driving me into the open palm of the other hand.

Ken was still on the ground, his sword embedded in the palm of the first hand—but he wasn't unarmed.

He hurled the boomerang.

It hit the first hand. On contact, the hand simply . . . stopped moving.

I didn't miss the window of opportunity. With a yell, I plunged my shortsword into it, again and again.

```
[Your party has killed a lesser hand.
 You have earned 280 experience points.]
```

Then I sidestepped a swing from the other hand, just barely.

Ken caught his boomerang on the return, then hurled it again. Once again, the hand froze on contact.

I went in swinging. This one recovered faster, forming a fist and punching at me, but I managed to dodge around one of the many blocks.

Unfortunately, at that moment, another hand appeared through one of the other walls.

Ken caught his boomerang again, then scrambled to his feet.

I jabbed the injured hand again. It vanished.

Another hand appeared on the opposite side of the room. "Uh, Ken?"

He rushed to me.

The hands floated closer, meeting with each other and balling into fists. Then, they pressed together.

I recognized the gesture. They were cracking their knuckles.

"Run?" I asked Ken.

"Run," he concurred.

We ran, straight for the other door.

The hands followed us with surprising speed, but once we made it through the open doorway, we were safe.

...From them, at least.

In my haste, I hadn't checked the compass and map.

The door behind us slammed shut.

Ahead of us stood a terrifying beast. Standing eight feet tall, it had a single massive horn on its serpentine head, thick scales, and powerful rending claws.

"Is that..."

"Yes, Yui. That's a dragon."

We had, unfortunately, walked straight into the boss room.

The dragon opened its jaws to greet us, but not in a polite, talking sort of way.

No, when it exhaled, three colossal balls of fire shot across the room toward us.

We scattered. The balls of flame impacted against the walls, exploding. Even outside of the blast radius, I could feel the tremendous heat they emitted.

I definitely didn't want to get hit by that.

Ken reacted quickly, hurling his boomerang. It hit the dragon dead-on in the forehead.

Tink.

It bounced off harmlessly.

Ken had a look of utter betrayal on his face as the boomerang flew back toward him.

I took a few steps forward. The dragon turned toward me, opening its jaws again.

Nope nope nope.

I hurled myself out of the way of another blast of flame.

Ken stared at his boomerang as he caught it. "Uh... I kind of left my sword in the last room..."

I tossed my sword to Ken, and he caught it deftly. Then, I unslung my bow just in time to avoid another blast of fire from the dragon. "Inventory. Remove arrow."

I nocked the arrow as it appeared in my hand. Ken advanced on the dragon with a look of grim determination, dodging another blast of flame, but only barely.

I loosed my arrow. It glanced harmlessly off the dragon's scales.

The dragon turned toward me, opening its jaws wide.

Ken lunged forward, trying to take advantage of its distraction.

It swung toward him, almost disdainfully, and smashed him with a single massive claw.

Ken flew back, blood trailing from his robes, and slammed into the back wall.

"Ken!" I yelled in panic. I retrieved another arrow from my Inventory.

"I'm... fine," he grunted, shifting on the ground. "Moderate

Heal." A brief glow surrounded him. He looked a little better, but he was still struggling to move.

The dragon turned toward him. I took aim and fired.

Again, the arrow bounced off harmlessly.

I let out a curse.

What can I do? Our weapons aren't working.

The dragon ignored my shot, maintaining its focus on Ken. It breathed again.

Ken, still on the ground, hurled his boomerang straight through the fiery breath. Then, with surprising dexterity, he tumbled across the ground in a roll, avoiding the fire.

The now-flaming boomerang struck the dragon . . . and still bounced right off.

Ken had to twist to avoid his own boomerang, which hit a wall and then quickly turned to ashes.

He had little time to look at it forlornly before the dragon opened his jaws again.

This isn't working. We need to hit it harder.

If we had Ken's sword . . .

I glanced back at the previous room. The door had slammed shut, but was that really a problem?

"Phase."

I rushed through the wall.

The two hands were waiting for me, but I blitzed right past them. They slammed into each other in my wake.

I grabbed the sword off the floor.

"Phase."

I ran through the wall, back into the dragon's room.

Ken was standing again, barely dodging another blast of fire. "You came back!"

"Catch!" I tossed him his sword. He caught it, passing my shortsword into his left hand.

"I'm going to distract it," I told him. "Hit it when it's vulnerable!"

Ken nodded. "Okay, but how—"

"Inventory. Remove arrow. Blink."

I reappeared in a corner of the room, right behind the dragon. I fired another arrow, aiming for an eye. It turned its head away in time but growled and turned back toward me. "Wait for it . . ."

Ken advanced slowly, a sword in each hand.

And I concentrated on something else in my Inventory.

A spiked block appeared behind me. I stood in its path.

I didn't know if it would move toward a dragon. But I did know that it would, most definitely, move toward me if I stood in front of its eyes.

The block flew through the air rapidly, almost too fast to dodge at close range. But I didn't have to move—not in the traditional way. I just had to speak.

"Blink."

I vanished.

And the block kept moving.

Massive spikes slammed straight into the dragon's chest. It howled in rage, spinning to look for me.

It found Ken instead, just as he lunged. His sword caught it just under the chin.

The dragon's head twisted upward, breathing fire into the ceiling. The room trembled around us.

HOW TO DEFEAT A DEMON KING IN TEN EASY STEPS

Ken struck again, with my own sword, managing another scratch.

And then the dragon turned down toward him. It was still alive, and his swords were stuck.

"Blink." I appeared right above the dragon, in midair. And then with a thought, I brought another spiked block out of my Inventory.

It fell straight down onto the dragon's head.

With a crack, the block smashed the dragon's head downward. The force of the impact jammed Ken's sword, still lodged in its neck, in deeper.

And then, with one final twitch on the ground, the dragon vanished.

[Your party has killed a small green dragon.
You have earned 3,981 experience points.]
[You have gained a level.]

There was only one room after the dragon's, but it was an important one.

A set of stairs led upward to an altar. And upon that altar laid a single glistening golden ring.

One of the five pieces of the Pentacrest, the legendary relic that would grant us entrance to the Demon King's palace.

I hesitated upon seeing it.

Was this really happening?

Was I worthy to take this step?

What would happen if I failed?

And then I thought back to that old man, waiting in the dungeon for a new Hero to come.

I thought of the people in the villages that had been destroyed by the Demon King's armies.

And I thought of the endless cycle of Heroes and Demon Kings, the violence that would bring ruin to the world time and time again.

Never again.

I may not be a Hero, but I will not wait and watch the world burn. I will not take comfort in the knowledge that the goddesses will send someone else to save us.

It may not be something I was chosen for, but I will make my own path. I will break the cycle.

And I will show this world that anyone can save it, if they try.

I strode forward, watching the softly glowing circle. It was beautiful. A sacred relic of legend, one I'd dreamed of a hundred times.

I whacked it with my sword a couple times. Nothing happened.

Ken shot me a withering glance.

I gave him a sheepish look in return, rubbing the back of my head. "Look, it could have been a mimic, okay?!"

"Just pick up the Pentacrest Piece, Yui."

I reached out and picked up the golden ring. It gleamed brightly in my hand, and I felt a sense of warmth and calm wash over me. For once, everything felt right.

"Let's go, Ken. We have a world to save."

STEP SEVEN

WAIT, YOU FORGOT TO RECRUIT LOYAL COMPANIONS, DO THAT

KEN HEALED OUR WOUNDS after the big fight, then we made our way back to the boss room. I carefully retrieved the two spike blocks that I'd used and stored them in my Inventory. They'd already helped us with one boss fight; I wasn't going to leave them behind.

After that, we did one last sweep through the dungeon for loot but didn't find much. I took a few more magic torches because I could.

It took close to three days to make it back to town after clearing the dungeon, but that wouldn't be a problem in the future. Because during the journey back, I'd chosen to take another level in Bag Mage, and I'd unlocked a new spell—Town Gate.

Town Gate would allow me to bind myself to an Ancestral Monument, a special type of structure infused with great magical power. Upon completing that binding, I would be able to cast Town Gate to open a gateway to that monument. I could then travel through it, and so could my allies. The portal would only last about a minute, and I could only be bound to one location at a time, but it was still an amazing spell.

If I'd had it during the fight with the dragon, perhaps I would have used it to flee. Fleeing might have been possible with Phase, but it would have been much trickier. That thing had been far too powerful for us to defeat without using tricks like the blocks, and it served as a grim reminder of how much deadlier bosses could be compared to ordinary monsters.

I wouldn't make the same mistake twice. We'd be better prepared before we went to the next dungeon.

After arriving, I immediately touched the gigantic stone monument in the center of the town. It glowed at my touch, indicating that I'd successfully bound my spirit to it. This would allow me to use my new Town Gate spell to return there quickly in the future.

I wished I'd obtained that spell before going to the dungeon. It would have made the trip back so much faster. I was exhausted.

Rather than going straight to bed, however, we decided to take some time at the nearby town inn to celebrate.

We grabbed a table by the fire, ordered food and more than a few drinks, and relaxed. We were both too exhausted to chat, but I enjoyed listening to the talks of the other adventurers nearby. They told tales of their own exploits and rumors of things happening around the world.

"Heard the Demon King's army hit another kingdom recently. If we're not lucky, we might be next!"

"Up, left, down, left is the way to the secret."

"Did you hear that Princess Fitzgerald disappeared a couple days ago? I wonder if it has anything to do with that dungeon someone cleared."

I perked up at that. The princess had disappeared? Had she been captured by the Demon King?

Wasn't it a little early for that?

Wait, was that our fault?

How did anyone even know we'd cleared that dungeon so soon? It had only been a few days. Had someone been watching us?

I gave Ken a look, but he didn't seem to be paying attention to the same conversation. He was too busy checking out a cute mage at another table.

I rolled my eyes and went back to my soup, pondering.

Was this really the right path?

Could I justify continuing on my self-made quest, knowing that I might fail and get people hurt in the process?

Somehow, the soup seemed colder when I took my next sip.

The night passed, and I found no easy answers.

In the morning, Ken pulled aside the curtains blocking the window, pouring light into our room. I groaned, pulling the rough sheets of my bed tighter and rolling into a ball. "Grm. Early."

Ken laughed and sat down at the foot of my bed. "Ah, precisely! Bright and early. Plenty of time to get things done."

"Mrgrg."

Truly, my mastery of articulate speech was my most heroic quality.

Ken patted my leg. "I'll go order breakfast."

I must have fallen back to sleep after that, because the next thing I remember was the smell of food and tea.

Cautiously and with the utmost skepticism, I peered out from beneath the covers. There was a tray of food sitting on a table next to me.

"Mm." I shivered, slowly dislodging myself from the sheets, and rubbed my eyes.

Ken pulled over another chair—I don't know when or where he got one; there had only been one in the room to start with—and sat down next to me, a plate on his lap. He delicately lifted a cup of tea and took a sip. "You should drink, at least. It'll help with the hangover."

"Mrm. Not hungover," I insisted. Not much, at least. I still took his advice and took a sip of the tea. It was hot and herbal, but I couldn't really enjoy it. There was too much on my mind.

"You seem glum, chum. What's bothering you?"

I frowned, letting out a sigh. "I'm not sure I should say anything."

"Come now, we've just had quite a victory together. If we are to be companions, we must share both the good and the bad, yes?"

I supposed he was right. "I'm just ... having reservations."

"Truly? You've always seemed quite steadfast. What bothers you so?"

"Well, I was listening to rumors last night, and I heard that the princess had disappeared."

"Ah, yes! Most likely captured. This adds such legitimacy to our quest!"

I blinked. "What?"

"Princess capturing is a grand tradition! If the Demon King has struck so soon, he truly must be acknowledging us. I'd think you'd be thrilled."

"She's a person, Ken. We could be getting her injured or killed!"

Ken frowned. "Well, I suppose. But don't you think that she'd be, well, ready for that? I imagine every princess in that family has been trained their entire life to be captured by the Demon King. It's sort of their lot in life. Prophecies and all that."

"That ... doesn't really make it any better. And wouldn't this princess normally be, well, out of season? There shouldn't be a Hero for more than seventy years. She probably thought she had an out." I shook my head. "And even if she was prepared, that wouldn't make it much better. Honestly, this whole prophetic cycle is garbage. Can you imagine being born and knowing that at some point, a Demon King was probably going to capture you just to play some role in a traditional story?"

Ken raised a hand to his chin, considering. "I suppose you may be right. If it's any consolation, though, the princess usually does get to shoot him in the heart with a golden bow and arrows of light toward the end of things. I imagine that will be quite cathartic for her!"

"That... doesn't really help, but thanks." I sighed. "What if we fail, and she just... dies? Because we had the audacity to start a quest without a true Hero? Or worse, what if by completing dungeons, we've deprived the next Hero of the resources he needs to succeed?"

"Well, the dungeons refill themselves between Heroes. I don't know how, but it always happens. I imagine that within the next seventy-odd years, they'll repopulate." He shook his head. "I began this journey with you knowing those risks. There may be consequences. Nay, there will be consequences. We may die, we may get others killed. But we must think, too, of the consequences of doing nothing. You are the one who once told me that you would not wait and watch while the world burned around you—is that not still true?"

I winced. "It is. Maybe. I don't know. I felt so certain when this all started, but seeing someone else get hurt because of me... it's not as easy as I expected."

Ken put a hand on my knee. "If watching others suffer was easy for you, you never would have taken this task in the first place.

You have empathy. Never lose that. It's the most important part of being a Hero." He raised a finger. "Well, that and the outfit. Which reminds me..."

I raised an eyebrow.

"You've been entirely underdressed for too long. Come here." Ken gestured to me, stood up from his chair, and walked over to his bed. Then he opened his backpack. "I went out early and purchased the last few things. And with a bit of a Fashionista's touch... it's finally ready."

He reached into the bag and withdrew the finished product, laying it down on the table near our beds.

A simple green tunic accompanied by a green archer's cap.

The traditional garb of a Hero.

I admit that my eyes teared up just a little. "I don't think I can take this. I'm not a real Hero."

He snorted at me. "Do you think you need a class to wear a fancy outfit?"

"I mean, maybe? I know armor requires proficiencies. I've only got light and medium."

Ken rolled his eyes. "This isn't heroic armor, dear. This is a Hero's Tunic and Hero's Hat. And while they will protect you, I assure you they have no proficiency requirements whatsoever. And they'll fit you perfectly. Both physically and in terms of your heroic demeanor."

"I don't know. I... still have doubts."

Ken walked over and sat down in front of me. "Aside from empathy and a perfect outfit, having doubts is the next most important part of being a Hero. Anyone who doesn't take the time to evaluate the consequences of their actions for others from time to time is taking the Demon King's path, not the Hero's. Now, try this on. I went to a lot of work to make this, and I'll be quite put out if you don't like it."

Ken was a little pushy, but he was right.

(Although I tried not to think about how he'd gotten my measurements. I was just hoping it was a Fashionista skill.)

The outfit fit perfectly over my existing leather armor. (I wasn't going to wear it without my armor—fashionable or not, a green tunic was no replacement for not dying.)

And just wearing the tunic and hat, as silly as it was, helped me regain my focus.

Maybe I didn't have to be perfect. Maybe there wasn't a perfect approach or a solution that didn't have consequences.

But I'd made a choice from the start. To fight. To try to save the world, even if no one else would.

I wasn't going to stop until I'd succeeded or given my very last breath.

We spent the next week doing what we did best—hunting an incredible number of slimes.

If we'd been a little more traditional, we probably would have moved up to fighting monsters more appropriate for our level. Orcs, maybe, or some mild demons. We'd conquered a dungeon, after all, and even slain a dragon. But me? I wasn't really much for needless challenges. Efficiency was more important. And that tangle with the dragon had shown me that I was still far from properly prepared for boss monsters.

Truthfully, it was a nice way to relax. The slimes no longer offered us any risk, and the metal ones still gave us considerable experience.

The princess herself wasn't my chief concern—thousands of people had died from the Demon King's invasion already, and a princess, no matter how royal, was no more valuable than any other person. No, the reason it worried me was that it was a form of escalation. Either the Demon King was aware that a dungeon had been conquered (which I considered eminently plausible), or he had simply chosen to advance the timetable of his conquest independently. Either was worrying, for different reasons.

By the end of the week, we'd managed to gain two more levels. Between that and the level we'd earned from the dragon, we were both Level 14.

I'd unlocked the Dragon Hunter class from killing the dragon. While leveling up was sincerely tempting, it had a lot of overlap with my existing Slime Hunter class, so I didn't pick it for now.

Instead, I focused entirely on my Bag Mage class. With two more levels in Bag Mage applied, I was up to Level 12 in Bag Mage and Level 2 in Slime Hunter.

I didn't get any new skills out of that, but I did pick up one more new Dimensional Magic spell, Gravity. It apparently would pull objects and people toward me, which seemed pretty useful. After a brief series of tests, I determined that it could pull someone as heavy as Ken (sorry, Ken) toward me, but slowly. It moved small objects much more quickly.

Ken was up to Level 11 in Sword Saint and Level 3 in Fashionista. I wasn't really sure what his logic was for that third Fashionista level, but getting to Level 11 in Sword Saint got him a Holy Slash ability, which sounded pretty good. Apparently, it was more like a special attack than a spell, using mana to cause holy damage on his next swing.

To celebrate our new levels, we went back to town and bought some upgraded equipment.

I finally bought myself a longsword, since I'd noted how important reach could be. I kept my shortsword, too, since my Ambidexterity skill would allow me to use weapons in both hands if I wanted to. I bought a large shield as well and stuck it in my Inventory, just in case I ran into an opponent I wanted to fight against more defensively.

Ken splurged on buying a sword made of magesilver, a legendary substance that was harder and lighter than steel. Apparently it was pretty good for conducting magic through, too, which would be useful for his Holy Slash skill and any similar skills he picked up later. I encouraged him to buy some armor, but he told me it clashed with his aesthetic.

Instead, he spent the rest of his money on buying a handful of powerful healing potions.

"I can heal with my magic, but this lets me save mana," Ken explained. "And they're also useful against certain types of monsters. Healing magic burns the undead and some types of demons. With a powerful-enough healing item or spell, you even destroy certain types of undead outright."

That gave me an idea.

I'd been focusing so much on traditional weapons and armor that I'd been neglecting to think of other items. Potions were useful, but there were other options for equipment that would come in handy.

With my remaining money, I purchased the most powerful magical item I could afford—a Lightning Rod. It was capable of calling down a blast of lightning utilizing the user's own mana. With it, it would be almost as if I could use offensive magic on my own.

That would be fantastic for opponents that were too tough for my bow to damage, or those rare monsters that were immune to physical damage entirely.

Unfortunately, with that purchase, I was completely broke.

With some new levels and better gear, we got back to strategizing.

I began with a modest proposal. "So, I was thinking, if we killed about a thousand more silver slimes—"

"Please, Yui, no. Have some mercy. Every time I go through that disgusting forest, I have to replace my entire outfit. If we spend one more day in that horrible place, I think I'm going to have to replace my skin." Ken gave a shudder.

I thought he was being a little melodramatic, but he had a point. That place was pretty icky. "Okay. But we very nearly died fighting the boss of the first dungeon, and I don't feel like even a couple levels and equipment upgrades are going to be enough to make us safe. Maybe we could go hunt something more dangerous? I heard about a place with giant silver slimes . . ."

"No more slimes, Yui. I don't care what size they are, how shiny they are, or anything else. No. More. Slimes."

I gave a sigh of resignation. "Okay, but ordinary monsters are going to be a lot harder."

HOW TO DEFEAT A DEMON KING IN TEN EASY STEPS

"To fight? Maybe. Harder on my complexion and wardrobe budget? Certainly not." Ken folded his arms.

I took a moment to ponder that. I hadn't really been looking for places to hunt that didn't involve exploiting my slime-hunting abilities for easy experience and loot. "Fine, fine. You're always rambling about what the Hero would need—what would the Hero have to help keep him safe that we're currently lacking?"

"Well, that depends in part on the specific Hero," Ken replied. "Many of the Heroes had legendary magic items that assisted them in their quests. Gauntlets that allowed the lifting of heavy rocks, finned shoes for swimming faster, a magic harmonica for playing songs to unlock certain hidden locations..."

"... How are finned shoes a magical item? Isn't that just, like, swimwear?"

"They're magic swimwear, Yui. Try to keep up."

I sighed. "Okay. Fine. Magic swimwear. What else?"

Ken clasped his hands together, his expression brightening. "Ah! I know what we're missing. I can't believe I didn't think of it sooner. There's something every Hero needs in case of emergencies."

I racked my brain to think of what Ken was talking about. There were some items that many Heroes used—swords, bows, green tunics... we'd covered most of that. There were a few that were defining features of specific Heroes, like the Timey-Wimey Hero using a harmonica, or the Wolf Hero somehow learning to shapeshift, but I couldn't think of a lot of other elements that all the Heroes had in common... except... "Please don't tell me this is going to be about explosives again."

Ken snorted. "Certainly not. No, we should get some bombs, but this is far more important. We—nay, you—need a faerie."

I stared at him. "No. You're joking."

"Yes!" He brightened. "It's so clear to me now! Every successful Hero has one. Or more. Some of them practically had hordes of faeries."

Now I folded my arms. "There's one pretty serious problem there—faeries are notoriously capricious. They're terribly difficult for anyone to deal with aside from the Hero. And Heroes don't always get along with them."

"But we do have a Hero, don't we? Look at how heroic you are! So green! So pristine!"

I sighed. "Please, Ken. Faeries live thousands of years. They're not going to be fooled into thinking I'm a Hero just because of an outfit."

I was confident about that, at least up until the point when we actually found a faerie several days later. I prepared to explain why we'd come to find her, but . . .

"Hero! You've come at last!" the winged maiden exclaimed, floating above the center of a tranquil, oddly rectangular-shaped pool of water. She was much larger than what I'd pictured of ordinary faeries—human height, with broad butterfly-like wings and wearing a long dress made of leaves. Her hair was bright green, but aside from that and the wings, she looked mostly human. "And my, aren't you a dashing one?" She gave me a wink.

Ken gave me an encouraging nudge, grinning brightly.

I took a deep breath, questioned my life choices for the hundredth time, and knelt in front of the pond. I had to stop myself from saying "thank you" and chose my words carefully. "You are quite lovely yourself."

Saying "thank you" could have implied that I owed the faerie something.

I wasn't an expert on dealing with faeries and their many rules and customs, but I'd learned bits and pieces during my studies of ancient Heroes—especially the Faerie Harem Hero and the Water Temple Hero—and I intended to avoid making any obvious mistakes if possible.

"From your obvious majesty, I can only presume that you are one of the Great Faeries. Is that correct?"

By "obvious majesty," I was actually just referring to her size. Ordinary faeries were barely larger than a palm—only the Great Faeries were human sized, as far as I knew.

She brightened. "Such flattery! I am, indeed, one of the Great Faeries—you may refer to me as Leafy Green. You're very kind. Can I keep you?"

"I'm afraid I have duties to attend to, and thus I cannot accept your generous offer. If you would be interested, however, I am currently on a journey to fight the Demon King, and I would be interested in your companionship."

Leafy Green gasped. "How exciting! I would absolutely love to see such a thing, but with matters being such as they are, I can't possibly leave this place for such a long quest. Too much to do, you see." She gestured toward the still pond. As far as I could tell, there was nothing in it—no fish, no other faeries swimming, not even algae. I had no idea if she was simply deflecting or if there was some actual mysterious faerie business she had to attend to down here.

I nodded slowly. "Well, if that's the case, how about assisting us with upgrading our equipment?" It was a long shot, but I'd heard that a couple of Heroes had gotten better weapons and shields simply by throwing their old ones in faerie ponds and waiting for a Great Faerie to throw out better ones in exchange. I had no idea why anything worked that way, but I wasn't going to pass up an opportunity for better gear if I could do it.

She tilted her head to the side, seemingly pondering. "I suppose if you want some faerie equipment, I could help with that... if you'd be willing to do me a favor in exchange. A favor that would work to both of our advantages."

I frowned. I didn't like where this was going. "What sort of favor?"

"Well, you're looking for a faerie, and I happen to know one that might be willing to go with you. She can be rather... difficult, however, and I would require you to persuade her to go with you— and to agree to take her through at least one dungeon, regardless of her actions. She needs it, the poor thing."

Ken slapped me on the shoulder.

"This sounds like an excellent plan! It's everything we wanted."

I glared at him a little.

Leafy Green ignored him entirely. "Well? Would you like to accept my deal?"

I took a deep breath, and with a feeling of great foreboding, I replied. "I'll... accept your deal."

"Wonderful!" Leafy Green flapped over to me, leaned over, and kissed me on the forehead. I felt something like a mild sting. "There we are, all sealed. Now, follow me, and I'll introduce you to Vex!"

"... Vex?"

Given that faerie names tended to be descriptive of their nature, I did not like the sound of that in the slightest.

Leafy Green led us across the Windswept Plains, through the Missing Forest, and all the way up a winding mountain path that didn't have any fancy name that I was aware of.

About halfway up the mountain, we found a river that flowed along the mountainside. We followed it for miles, until Leafy Green stopped in front of a waterfall. "We're here!"

"Here...?" Ken asked.

It was a subtle thing, but looking at the waterline, I could see an area that was much shallower than the rest of the river—shallow enough to walk across, if I didn't mind getting my boots a little wet. And, on the other side of the river, there was a narrow path... right up to the waterfall.

Leafy Green looked at us expectantly.

With growing concern, I stepped across the narrow, partly submerged river path. *My boots are going to be making that annoying squelching sound for days.*

Then, I carefully navigated the thin path on the opposite side until I reached the waterfall. I looked at it dubiously. Leafy Green just smiled at me.

I stared at it, then after a moment, I tentatively stuck my hand through the waterfall—and found a dry section on the other side.

Leafy Green smiled even brighter, flapping closer.

I stuck my head through the waterfall.

On the opposite side, I found the entry to a rough-hewn cavern. In spite of the natural appearance of the cave, there were a pair of torches glowing on the walls. I thought I heard a subtle musical tone as I glanced inside.

I mentally kicked myself for not expecting it. Of course there was going to be a secret passage behind a waterfall—there were always secret passages behind waterfalls.

I pushed through the waterfall and into the cavern beyond. The water soaked me on the way through, which wasn't ideal, but I warmed myself at one of the magical torches.

"Marvelous! Simply marvelous! A hidden faerie retreat!" Ken clapped his hands, tiny droplets of water flying from them on impact. "Shall we proceed?" He gestured toward the rest of the cave.

Leafy Green flew in behind us. Somehow, in spite of passing straight through the waterfall, not a single droplet of water hung off of her. "I'll go up ahead and knock. Vex is, uh, liable to be somewhat cranky at first. She's probably sleeping, and it takes her a while to wake up properly."

"How long is a while?" I asked.

"Oh, just a year or two." Leafy Green waved a hand dismissively. "It depends on how long she's been asleep, but I made her get up and stretch a few decades ago, so it shouldn't be too bad."

I groaned, already regretting my agreement. "Let's go."

We followed Leafy Green down the cavern. Fortunately, there were no monsters or traps, just a surprisingly long cavern that led to a large wooden door with intricate runes glowing on it.

I expected those runes meant that Leafy Green would have to

do something magicky to open the door. Instead, she just pounded on it loudly. "Wake up! Wake up!"

"Aaah!" came a smaller voice from the other side. "What is wrong with you?! I was sleeping!"

Leafy Green scoffed. "Yeah, that's all you do. Come on out, you've got visitors."

"Don't wanna. Leave me alone. I'm going back to bed." A tiny, adorable-sounding yawn came from the other side of the door. It was a stark contrast to the irritated tone of her voice.

Leafy Green folded her arms. "You come out here right now, young lady. There are human guests waiting for you!"

The other voice, presumably Vex, sounded positively vitriolic when she responded. "Ugh, that's even worse. Why would you bring humans here? They're the actual worst! Just go away already!"

"Don't make me come in there, young lady."

"Like you even could! I warded the door! Hmpf!"

Leafy Green leaned toward the door. "You will come out here this instant!"

"Stop bossing me around! You're not my mom!"

"You're an anthropomorphized concept, young lady. You don't have a mother."

"You take that back!"

This sort of back-and-forth went on for some time, before Leafy Green turned back toward us, giving a hopeless shrug. "Forgive Vex's impetuousness. She's still a teenager."

I blinked. "Didn't you say she'd been sleeping for decades?"

Leafy Green nodded. "Oh, yes. By teenager, I mean she's just over eighteen hundred years old. Practically still a child, and she still acts like one."

That made a surprising amount of sense. "... And you want me to try to talk to her?"

"That would be part of the agreement, yes." Leafy Green gestured toward the door.

I walked up to it, uncertain on how to even begin to try to coax a hostile teenaged faerie out of her room. Honestly, I wasn't even sure success at that would be a good thing in the long run.

Still, I hadn't gotten this far just to give up. If I could actually get a faerie to help, she'd be an invaluable resource... if she wasn't so insufferable that she cut our life expectancy more than she added to it.

"Hello, Vex? I'd like to talk to you, if you're willing."

A moment of silence. "What do you want, human?"

"I'm going on a dangerous journey, you see, and I could use the help of a..."—I hesitated a moment—"... talented faerie such as yourself."

"Uh-huh. Sure. And where is this dangerous journey leading?"

I glanced from side to side. Leafy Green gave me a two-handed gesture that I assumed was supposed to be encouraging.

I turned back to the door. "To the Demon King. I'm going to fight him."

"The Demon King." Vex's tone was matter-of-fact.

"Yes. You see, I—"

The door swung wide open. It was a human-sized door, so I'm still not quite sure how the six-inch-tall faerie on the other side managed to get it open.

HOW TO DEFEAT A DEMON KING IN TEN EASY STEPS

Either way, Vex was a hand-sized bundle of pissed. She had her fists raised, her jaw tight, and spheres of black energy rotated in the air around her. The only thing darker than the magic surrounding her was the black of her eyeliner.

"How. Dare. You." Vex pulled back a diminutive arm.

In the background, I noticed Leafy Green subtly slinking away.

I lifted my hands up in a warding gesture. "I didn't mean to offend, I just thought—"

"You thought, what? That it would be funny to get my hopes up? To pretend to want me, only to turn me aside like used garbage, just like he did?"

I briefly pondered asking why she'd said "used garbage" and what unused garbage might have entailed, but thankfully I thought better of it.

"I sincerely have no idea what you're talking about."

"Wait . . ." Ken made a contemplative expression. "This is all jogging my memories a bit. Oh! You're the Faerie Who Failed, aren't you?"

Vex turned toward him, and for a moment, I worried that her stare alone would strike him dead on the spot.

". . . Right. That was rude of me. Uh, could we, perhaps, forget I said anything? I'm just going to, uh . . ." Ken stepped behind me, apparently trying to hide. This was not very effective, since Ken was taller and wider than I was.

Vex visibly trembled with rage. "You . . . you're even wearing some kind of . . . sick mockery of his outfit, aren't you?"

Honestly, I'd been feeling pretty good about my green tunic

up to that point. "Hey, now. Ken worked really hard on this outfit. There's no need to be rude about it."

Vex narrowed her eyes at me, then hissed. "You come to my home, wearing that, and ask me to come with you to fight the Demon King? Did she put you up to this?"

We turned toward Leafy Green. She'd stopped subtly slinking and had started sprinting back down the tunnel away from us. I thought I heard her cackle along the way.

"Sort of."

Vex turned toward the fleeing figure, her wings fluttering. I stepped in the way before she could pursue, then raised my hands in a defensive gesture.

"I think we started off wrong here. I'm Yui. I'm not teasing you. I am, in fact, actually going after the Demon King. And I didn't know about your... particular background before coming here."

"It's her fault, then. She's always trying to get me to come out, luring me with false hope and broken promises. Just like his. There's nothing left out there for me. I... I can't." She dropped her hands, and I could sense her mood lower along with them. "Not again."

I'd heard about the Faerie Who Failed, of course. I'd just never known she still existed. She was a part of one of my favorite stories as a child.

You see, I always loved tragedies.

The Faerie Who Failed was the loyal companion to the Water Temple Hero. Who was, if you recall, one of only two Heroes in recorded history who failed to defeat the Demon King—and the only one who didn't even reach him. He disappeared in the Water Temple, his fate unknown.

HOW TO DEFEAT A DEMON KING IN TEN EASY STEPS

But worse than that, his faerie survived. She'd fled the Water Temple.

Such was a fate worse than death for a faerie bound to a Hero. She was sworn to sacrifice her life for her Hero if necessary—that was the pact struck between faeries and Heroes long ago. In surviving, she'd earned herself a moniker and a legend almost as infamous as the Water Temple Hero himself.

And like the ancient Heroes, though her true name had long faded into obscurity, her title and story remained.

I was quickly realizing that Leafy Green had far more than just sending a faerie along with us in mind. This was an intervention. Not a trick or a prank—it was a chance for a fallen faerie to earn redemption.

And I wasn't sure I could give it to her.

So, understanding that, I had to be honest with her. "Vex, listen to me. I understand if you don't want to go with me. I don't know what happened to you the last time you went after the Demon King"—her eyes burned as she turned her head up toward me—"but I know that this time is going to be different, one way or another. For one thing, I'm not even a real Hero. Not in the traditional sense."

Ken frowned at me. "Yui, wait. Maybe you shouldn't . . ."

"No, I'm not keeping a secret about something like this from someone we want to work with. Vex, I don't know if you're keeping track, but we're still many years away from a traditional Hero rising. I don't have the Hero class. But I've already cleared a dungeon, and I intend to clear the rest."

Vex turned her head to the side. "Why? That's not your job. That's what the Hero does."

"Because if everyone in this world waits for another Hero to save them, I don't know if this world will survive. And if I'm content to wait and let another person risk their life for me, I don't know if I'm worth saving."

Vex floated closer, looking conflicted. "Can you do it?"

"I don't know. But if Heroes can fail"—she winced when I said those words—"then maybe, just maybe, people who aren't Heroes can succeed. Maybe rather than leaning on prophecies and cycles, we should try to do things ourselves."

"You sound just like him." Vex's voice was barely a whisper.

"What do you mean?" I hadn't expected that response.

"He was so optimistic. He wanted to make a change. Break the cycle. He planned something ambitious, but in the end . . ." She shook her head sadly.

"Do you blame him for trying to do something different?" It was a painful question to ask, but important.

"No," she replied softly. "He was right all along. And until now, I thought he was the only one."

As she fluttered closer, I realized there were tiny teardrops dripping from her eyes.

"Vex, I don't know if I can be like that Hero, or any Hero at all. But if I'm to have any chance of success, I'm going to need a faerie's help, and I'd like it to be you. Will you come with me?"

She let out a ragged breath, half sobbing, and then floated closer to kiss me on the forehead. This time, I didn't feel a sting, but rather like ice cold had been pressed against me. "I will." She paused. "But I'm still really tired. You don't happen to have a glass bottle, by any chance, do you?"

"A glass bottle? Why?"

Ken shrugged at me. "Traditional traveling faerie habitat. She can sleep inside."

I stared at Ken, then at Vex. "Wouldn't you suffocate?"

"You have to make holes for air, obviously. And make sure the cork on the top isn't too secure. I need to be able to get out right when you're almost about to die."

After further discussion, it became clear that Vex was dead serious about the whole bottle thing.

We went back to town and got a bottle. I made sure there were ample air holes, and an easily removable top.

And with that, I had earned myself a faerie companion.

Don't think I let Leafy Green get away without delivering on her side of the bargain, by the way.

Right after securing Vex, we traveled back to Leafy Green's pond. She didn't show herself immediately, but she surfaced from the water (still appearing to be completely dry) as soon as I tossed a sword in.

"You want me to bless this piece of junk?" she asked.

"I mean, if you want to replace it with something better . . ." I nudged.

"No, it's fine. I'll bless what you have. A deal is a deal. Toss in anything you want to have blessed."

". . . Anything?"

About ten minutes later, Leafy Green collapsed on the side of the pool. "Please . . . mercy . . ."

A gigantic sack of recently blessed equipment was sitting next to her.

It would seem that in her haste to get us to take Vex, Leafy Green may have neglected to put a limit on the number of items she would bless for us. And, given how that scenario had played out, it was something I fully intended to take advantage of.

I didn't strictly need faerie-upgraded undergarments, nor did I know if they actually provided me with any additional defense or utility, but I wasn't going to turn down any potential edge I could get.

Especially after she called my sword "junk."

After Ken and I finished having her bless a simply ludicrous supply of items, we finally bid her goodbye.

For the moment, I fully intended to come back to get her to bless more "junk" later. She hadn't specified a time or quantity limit either.

In the meantime, however, I had other priorities. It was time to deliver on the second part of the deal—taking Vex through a dungeon.

STEP EIGHT

OKAY, NOW CLEAR THE REMAINING DUNGEONS IN THE PROPER ORDER

THERE WAS A TRADITIONAL sequence for clearing dungeons. Not every Hero followed it, but some dungeons were much easier than others—or provided equipment that would be useful in the next dungeon.

The gods had clearly stacked things in the Hero's favor, at least in some respects. But we'd run into a small problem that had me questioning whether going to the traditional second dungeon next was the wisest course of action.

There was a high chance that the Demon King already knew I'd cleared one of the dungeons. I couldn't guarantee it—maybe Princess Fitzgerald's disappearance was unrelated to the Demon King and/or unrelated to my dungeon clearing. I wasn't egocentric enough to think that literally everything happening was because of me.

But if I presumed that there was a chance the Demon King knew what I'd done, I had to make adjustments. I didn't know if he'd be concerned about non-Heroes, but I could at least be cautious.

So, rather than going to the next and most convenient dungeon immediately, I chose to make a somewhat less predictable move.

Ken and I headed straight for the Water Temple, the most notorious and dangerous of all dungeons. It had a legendary reputation for wickedness.

It was where the strongest Hero of all had disappeared, never to return.

On the way to the Water Temple, we encountered a strange figure on the road.

They were sitting on a rocky outcropping just off the path, playing soft music on some kind of a musical instrument. At first, I didn't recognize that it was a harmonica, like the ones that several legendary Heroes were known to play.

The figure was covered head to toe in black robes, with some stylized golden threading across the shoulders. They wore a scarf, as well as a cloth mask that covered the lower half of their face, and an eye patch over their right eye. Two knives sat on their hips, each with a distinctive gold-winged pommel. I couldn't tell if they were male or female; they were skinny, with an athletic build, and very few of their features were visible.

Ken and I warily approached.

The figure finished playing the last notes of their melody—one that seemed somewhat familiar—and turned to look down at us.

"Greetings, Hero." The figure hopped down from the rock, landing dramatically in the center of the road. Their voice, much like their appearance, was androgynous. As they landed, they tossed their scarf backward with a flourish. It would have been quite impressive if they hadn't hit themselves in the face with it and stumbled a few steps after the landing.

That didn't stop them from continuing to talk as if nothing had happened, though.

"So, Hero, you've finally made it here. The Water Temple."

I blinked. "I'm sorry, not actually the H—"

Ken covered my mouth. "Yes, we're here. Sorry for taking so long. How may we help you?"

The masked figure raised a single eyebrow, then replied. "The Water Temple is sealed, as it has been since the coming of the last Hero. I am here to assist you with opening it."

"That is so very nice of you, thank you. I'm Ken, by the way, and this is the Hero, Yui." Ken flashed the masked figure a smile.

I pushed Ken's hand away from my mouth with a groan. "Yes. Nice to meet you. I liked your song."

I think the figure blushed slightly at my remark. "It . . . it was nothing. I mean, um, it was, I was playing it for you. Because, you know, you need to know it."

Ken nodded seriously, as if he knew what the masked figure was talking about. "It is a sacred song, then?"

I'd heard of those. Legendary songs passed down to the Hero from the royal family or the great sages, each with magical power.

"Indeed, Ken." The masked figure gave him a nod. "You are wise, and worthy to be a companion of the Hero."

Ken preened a little bit. "Ah-hah-ha. Of course."

I resisted the urge to roll my eyes. "Thank you, that's very kind of you. I don't suppose you could tell us who you are, or how you knew we were going to be here? Are you one of the descendants of the sages, perhaps?"

"Hmpf." The figure crossed their arms. "I am nothing. No one. Simply a wandering ninja, and definitely not a princess of the royal family."

I raised an eyebrow. "That's, uh, weirdly specific, but sure. Okay. Do you have a name, or am I just supposed to call you 'Definitely Not a Princess'?"

The supposed ninja narrowed their single visible eye. "If you must give me a name ... you may refer to me as ... Nameless Kage."

"You want your name to be ... Nameless. That's, uh, sort of a cont—"

Ken covered my mouth again. "We are honored to meet you, esteemed Nameless Kage. Alas, we were down the road when you began the song and were not able to hear the entirety of it. Would you be kind enough to play it again?"

"Of course. Such is my duty as a prin ... er, ninja. Music-playing ninja. Yes." Nameless raised the harmonica to their lips and began to play.

I took a moment to relax, listen, and bask in the music.

Ken clapped when they finished. "Excellent! Wonderful!" He turned to me. "Did you memorize that?"

"We've been over this, Ken. I don't play the flute, the harmonica, or any other sort of wind instrument."

"Impossible." Nameless stepped forward. "You cannot progress in your quest without playing the harmonica."

Ken gave me a look. "Told you we should have got you one, Yui."

"Hey, look, I can't do everything."

"It is your job, Hero, to do everything," Nameless explained. "It is your great strength, and your burden. I do not envy you. Fear not, however. If you do not yet have the skill to play the harmonica, you still have many years before the Demon King conquers these lands. You may only have to bear the deaths of tens, perhaps hundreds of thousands of people on your conscience as you flounder throughout your quest without the necessary skills to succeed."

"Wow, gosh, if you put it like that, maybe I should have taken up the harmonica. Yeah, thanks for that reassurance, Nameless." I sighed. "Couldn't you, you know, just go with us and play the relevant songs for us?"

The "ninja" let out a gasp, raising a hand to their chest. "Why, of course not! That would be unheard of. A prin—ah, ninja, would never make a viable companion to the Hero. I am simply not suited for such a thing. I must teach you the song, then vanish into obscurity until such a time I am needed to make a dramatic entrance."

"Our esteemed Nameless friend is right, Yui." Ken nodded. "The precedent is clear here."

I gave an exasperated sigh. "Couldn't you learn to play the harmonica, Ken, since you're so keen on the idea?"

"Absolutely not. What happens when we're separated in the final dungeon by the four Demon Generals, and you're forced to go on and confront the Demon King alone?"

"I was thinking we'd, uh, you know, maybe avoid that?"

There were gasps from both of the others.

I sighed. "Never mind. Look, Nameless Ninja."

"Kage," they corrected.

"Right. Nameless Kage, which is definitely not a name, who is also a ninja and most certainly not a princess."

They nodded at my correction.

"Aaaanyway, given that I don't have a harmonica or any idea to use one, perhaps you could take some time to teach it to me, and then loan me your harmonica?"

They hesitated. "I don't know . . . This is something of an heirloom of the royal family . . ." They didn't even seem to notice the implication there.

"Okay. Fine. I'm going back to town and buying a dirt-cheap

harmonica. Then, you can give me some lessons, and I'll go murder some silver slimes and take a level in Performer or Minstrel or something to make sure I don't mess it up."

Nameless Kage looked wary. "Your levels in the Hero class should be sufficient to give you all the skills you need."

"I don't actually—"

Ken covered my mouth again. "Our Hero is, indeed, a strange one. She's, uh, new at this. But an excellent Hero, I assure you!"

"...She?" Nameless squinted her one visible eye at me. "Wait a moment, is that right...? I just assumed you were a young lad, what with your short hair and athletic build. Shouldn't the Hero be—?"

"Hah ha!" Ken slapped me on the back. "There is nothing to worry about, friend Nameless. Surely you can see that Yui is wearing a green tunic."

Nameless squinted again, then nodded. "Yes."

"And the Hero is known to wear a green tunic, yes?"

Nameless nodded. "Indeed. It is so. The legends passed down in my family are quite clear on this point."

"And look!" Ken pointed at me. "A green hat as well! And see this? A sword, and a bow! Truly, a finer Hero could not be hoped for."

I glared at Ken.

He grinned brightly.

Nameless tilted their head to the side, then drew in a breath and bowed at the waist. "Forgive me, Hero. I was a fool to have ever doubted you. Your loyal companion has convinced me of the error in my judgment."

"It's, uh, fine. Thanks, Nameless Prin—uh, Kage."

Nameless stood back up and nodded. "Given that you have not

been taught the ways of the harmonica yet, and will need some time to purchase one—"

"Won't be long at all, actually. Town Gate."

A glimmering portal appeared behind me.

Nameless stared. "Are Heroes supposed to be able to do that?"

"Ah-ha-ha." Ken stepped forward. "Truly, our Hero is a cut above the rest, yes? So fresh and versatile!"

Nameless hesitated, then nodded gravely. "Indeed. It is so."

"So, I'll just go get that harmonica, and then we can start the lessons, I guess?"

Nameless nodded. "I see. Yes, this is good. You may not see me when you return, however. Call out if I appear to be missing... for I will be one with the shadows."

With that, Nameless pulled out something from a pouch and hurled it to the ground. A blast of smoke shot up as the vial cracked, concealing Nameless.

Just for a moment, though. We could very clearly see them attempting to run around a corner after the wind blew the smoke away.

When they got around the bend, I thought I heard them trip over something.

"Should we check on them, or...?" I asked Ken.

"Oh!" Ken yelled, "Where did Nameless vanish to? Such amazing ninja skills!"

I sighed. "Really?"

"Play along. It's clearly important to them."

I paused for a moment, then yelled, "Wow, I have no idea. Truly, they vanished without a trace."

Never mind the muddy footprints leading around the corner. It looked like their boots were wet or something. Maybe they'd gotten them drenched in the water outside the temple somehow?

"Good." Ken nodded to me. "Shall we go back to town now?"

"Let's get this over with."

We returned to town via the portal, obtained a harmonica, and then went back and found Nameless easily.

I began my harmonica lessons.

It was terrible.

Nameless was a good and patient teacher, but without any relevant skills, my music was... let's just say "not good" and be done with that.

Fortunately, practice was all it took to unlock the prerequisites for a class.

I spent the next few days taking trips to the Water Temple to meet with Nameless for lessons, then going back to the forest to hunt more silver slimes.

Ken begged and pleaded for us to find somewhere—anywhere—else to hunt, but slimes were simply too convenient.

After about a week and the loss of one more of Ken's entire wardrobe sets, we'd accomplished our goal.

[You have gained a level.]

I'd finally reached Level 15. And with some regret, I spent that level on the Bard class.

[You have gained the Perform skill.]

HOW TO DEFEAT A DEMON KING IN TEN EASY STEPS

[You have gained the Song Magic skill.]
[You have learned the Song of Slumber.]

I wasn't particularly thrilled with any of that, but at least a new type of magic was neat.

Once I had the Perform skill, practice increased that skill rapidly.

Within a few more days, I'd reached the point where my basic musical skills were passable.

It didn't take long after that before I finally reaped the benefits of Nameless's training.

[You have learned Song Specifically for Unlocking the Water Temple.]

And, perhaps more important, that wasn't the only song Nameless taught me.

[You have learned the Song of Weather.]
[You have learned the Song of Spirits.]
[You have learned the Song of Faerie Calling.]
[You have learned the Song Passed Down to Members of the Royal Family.]

Maybe this wasn't such a waste of time after all.

The Water Temple was a colossal structure of white stone, wrought in an age when magic was more widespread and people were poor at predicting when certain sites would eventually end up completely underwater.

It wasn't always the Water Temple, you see. That's just what happens when you build a big structure on a small scenic island that isn't structurally sound. Eventually it sinks, and you want to make it sound like it was your idea all along.

Anyway, the most important part is that the Water Temple was underwater. It was in the center of a small circular lake, maybe a few hundred feet in diameter. There was still a road leading up to what once was the entrance, but it ended at a sheer cliff. I could see the former entrance about twenty feet below.

Ken stared out at it. "You know, Yui, I appreciate your . . . um, let's call it nonstandard approach to solving dungeons. But we can't breathe underwater, and that place is, well, entirely underwater."

"That's what the song is for, yeah?" I lifted my harmonica.

Ken winced as I lifted it to my lips. I felt mildly offended. I wasn't that bad at playing music, was I? It's possible that a few weeks of music practice wasn't exactly enough to make me an inspiring performer, true. But I had natural talent! At least, that's what I like to tell myself so I can forget the horror on his face every time I tried to play something.

"The song will get us through the front door, yes, but . . ."

"Then we'll work from there!" I beamed, ever optimistic about plunging into the depths of things far beyond my level of skill or knowledge.

Then I raised the harmonica and played the legendary Song Specifically for Unlocking the Water Temple.

As I finished the song, I heard something like a strange string of musical notes in the air, then felt a deep rumble within the ground.

The gigantic metal doors of the temple trembled, then opened wide. I'd successfully unsealed the temple. That was just the beginning, though.

HOW TO DEFEAT A DEMON KING IN TEN EASY STEPS

I watched in fascination as a series of pillars rose from the floor of the lake below, forming steps leading to the entrance of the temple. An entrance which was, unfortunately, still underwater.

"I can work with that."

I hopped to the first pillar, then the second. There were small gaps between them, but they were easy enough for Ken and I to manage.

"I really don't think we're ready for this one, Yui. According to legend, we're lacking the proper tools. See that ring on the pillar up ahead?" Ken pointed at one of the pillars.

I could see the ring he was talking about—it was toward the middle of the pillar, and roughly large enough for one hand to grip. "Sure, why?"

"That's for a grappling hook launcher, one of the legendary Hero's tools. We don't have one."

I frowned. "Is . . . that really a problem? I have a normal rope and grappling hook in my Inventory."

Ken shook his head disdainfully. "That's completely different. According to legend, the Hero's grappling hook launcher is a device that fires a grappling line like a crossbow."

"That . . . just sounds like an ordinary tool, Ken. Is it like, magical or something?"

"I honestly have no idea. But I'm confident that's what the rings are for. No grappling launcher, no rings, no completing the Water Temple."

I sighed. "You're too worried about little things like that. I'm sure we'll work it out. Come on."

Ken frowned but continued jumping with me. Eventually, we reached a pillar that was just at the waterline. This one was different from the others. It had strange glyphs cut into a runic pattern all over the center of it.

They were interesting, but I couldn't read them, so I focused on the problem at hand.

I knelt down at the waterline, thinking. In the back of my mind, I was half aware of Ken giving another historical lecture.

"Why, this series of patterns was carved in the era of the Faerie Harem Hero! It must be eight hundred years old... Now, in those times, the Hero was known for..."

Blah blah blah. Ken kept talking. I got to work.

I put my hand up against the waterline. It was time for an important test.

"Now, the Water Temple is supposed to have three different places to raise and lower the water level... they're like switches."

"Mm-hm." I gave a noncommittal reply, not really paying attention.

My plan was already working. A little slower than I would have liked, but that made sense. I dipped my arm in deeper.

"If we can figure out the right song to play at each, then we might have a chance to make it through this place, even without underwater breathing gear. Which, by the way, we definitely should have."

"Yep, should have," I echoed, still not paying attention.

"If I remember my legends right, we can obtain water-breathing items from the merfolk just north of here. Now, my merfolk language skills are a little rusty, but..."

I jumped in the water. Couldn't keep working without doing it that way—the water had already dipped below the level I could reach with my arm from the top of the pillar after all.

When I came back to the surface, Ken was gawking at me.

"Yui. What have you done?!"

You see, when I came back up for air, the water level was several feet lower than before. Lower, in fact, than the entrance to the Water Temple. We had a path now.

I grinned. "Fixed the temple entrance problem. Shall we—"

"No, Yui. No. What. How?"

I raised a hand, grinning and pointing a finger at him. "Secondary Inventory. Release one unit of water."

Gallons of stored water flowed out from my fingertip in an instant, and with surprising force. Not literally from the finger, of course, but from my Inventory, which contained about a half million gallons of lake water.

That might sound improbable, but let me explain.

At Level 100 in Bag Magic, I'd unlocked Ultimate Inventory Capacity.

With Superior Inventory Capacity, I'd been able to store a large water drum's worth of water in one slot. Those held about fifty or sixty gallons, and didn't quite push my slot to capacity, which I estimated to be about a hundred gallons. I just hadn't found any water barrels with that size to test.

Now, with Ultimate Inventory Capacity, I could store ten times that in a single slot. I hadn't found any drums of water of that size, but when storing liquid without a container, I found that it worked just like I'd hoped. I estimated that I could store about a thousand gallons of water in a single Inventory slot.

With Bag Magic at Level 100, I now had four hundred Inventory slots. And with the Double Bag skill, I had a second Inventory with another four hundred slots. So, eight hundred slots total, each of which could hold a thousand gallons of water.

I hadn't drained the entire lake into my Inventory, but I'd managed a good part of it. And I still had a bit of Inventory room left to spare.

Bag Magic really is pretty powerful, isn't it?

Anyway, math aside, Ken barely managed to yelp and jump to the side of my sudden jet of a thousand gallons of water flying in his direction.

He glared down at me, folding his arms. "You put the sacred lake back where it belongs right now."

"Don't wanna." I stuck my tongue out at him. If he was going to talk to me like I was a child, I'd play along.

"That water is blessed, Yui! It burns demons and undead! It's the only thing that keeps the Demon King from entering this place!"

I shrugged at him. "I can put some of it back later. For now, this is the easiest way to handle the dungeon."

Ken continued to glare. I swam to the temple doors, pulling myself up onto the stone floor, and then looked back toward him. "You coming?"

With a deep breath and a wrinkle of his nose, Ken replied. "Fine. But you're putting the sacred lake back when we're done here."

"I make no such promises."

The interior of the Water Temple was, predictably, pretty damp.

While there had been large doors to seal the entrance, the inside of the temple had also been submerged in water. The doors had, presumably, just been keeping non-Heroes from robbing the place.

And given our current plans, not very effectively.

I advanced slowly, noting the magic torches that ignited on the walls as we passed down the first hall.

Did those work underwater? I presumed they had to, given that this hall was expected to be underwater . . . but maybe the place had just been badly designed.

Either way, I was glad it wasn't pitch dark ahead.

Ken put a hand on my shoulder to stop me before I advanced out of the entry hall and into the first room. "Yui. Listen. If we're really doing this, I need you to pay attention to me for a moment."

Given the seriousness of his tone, I paused and turned to talk to him. "Okay."

"First off, we should ask Vex what she remembers about the place, and how the Water Temple Hero died in here."

I nodded. I still had Vex in a bag at my side . . . which, I belatedly realized, had air holes in it.

Which were also water holes. And when I'd been swimming, that bag had been submerged.

After a moment of panic, I tore the bottle out of my bag. Vex popped the top off of it, poking her head above the water that was now filling the entire bottle. "That was a nice swim. What's the occasion?"

I gave a little cough. "Were you . . . uh, okay in there?"

"Hm? Oh, sure! I can breathe underwater for hours." Vex stared at me. "Wait, you didn't know that and you jumped into the water?"

I gave her an abashed look. "I, uh . . . you could have gotten out if you needed to, right?"

Vex shrugged. "Probably. Unless I, you know, drowned in my sleep or something."

Ken gave me a hard look.

I winced. "I'll, uh, be more careful. So, don't freak out, but we're in a dungeon now."

"Oh yeah?" Vex brightened. "That's great! Which . . . one . . . ?"

She trailed off as she began to turn her head and inspect the walls, and apparently, revelation struck her. She spoke again before I had a chance to explain. "No. You didn't."

"I . . . uh . . . surprise?"

The next several moments were filled with Vex screaming.

After the screaming stopped, I took a moment to evaluate just how bad my decisions leading up to that situation had been.

The verdict: really bad.

But there was a silver lining. The doors to the temple had slammed shut behind us just after the screaming started, and now we had no choice but to go inside!

(Well, I obviously could have cast Town Gate. But I wasn't going to remind Ken or Vex that I could do that, since it worked better for my plans if we pressed on.)

"Okay. Breathe, Vex, breathe. Find your center. You can murder these humans when you feel better," Vex told herself.

I was not comforted by that, but she did seem to be calming down. I gave her a couple minutes.

"We are terribly, terribly sorry about not informing you about this earlier, Vex," Ken said, sounding sincere.

Vex only glared at him.

HOW TO DEFEAT A DEMON KING IN TEN EASY STEPS

"So . . . I suppose this might be a bad time to ask . . . but do you remember anything about this place?"

"Oh, I certainly do, thank you for asking, Yui. You see, I've been having nightmares, both waking and sleeping, about what happened here for the last several hundred years. Thanks for bringing me back here, really owe you one there."

I deserved that. "Do you want to leave?"

Vex glared at me. "You know what? No. Let's do this. Let's get my humans killed again. It'll be fun to see more people die in front of me, right in the same place as before."

Ken whispered to me. "I get the impression Vex isn't being entirely honest with that statement."

I hung my shoulders. "Look, Vex. I'm sorry. But we did have to go here eventually, and—"

"Forget it. I know. You want to fight the Demon King. Fine. Go right ahead. You can do it without any tips from me. I'm going back to sleep." Vex dove back into her bottle, folding her arms and submerging herself underwater.

I stuck a finger into the bottle and drained the water into my Inventory—even if she could breathe underwater for a while, I didn't want to risk her drowning eventually—then replaced the top and put her back in my bag.

I turned back to Ken. "Did you have other things to tell me, before I make any further mistakes?"

"Yes, actually. There should be two more ways to raise and lower the water here. We should keep our eyes open for them. And beyond that, there's something very important you should know."

I raised an eyebrow. "Oh?"

"This place is more than just a normal dungeon. It is a focal point for the divine power of the Silver Goddesses. At the center of the temple, we will find the last of the living Sacred Silver Trees. It's said that a true believer who touches the tree can seek their blessing there."

I remembered the burned-out Sacred Tree that had served as the entrance for the previous dungeon we'd explored. "I didn't know any of the trees had survived."

"I can't say for certain it has, but we were taught that the last of the Sacred Silver Trees was preserved here. Presumably, the temple being underwater made it more difficult for the Demon King to reach. Or perhaps the goddesses simply protected this whole place once the Demon King began burning the other trees to the ground."

That made a degree of sense. I wondered if, perhaps, the sinking of this island might not have been a coincidence. Could the goddesses have sunk the temple to keep the last of the sacred trees safe?

That was potentially useful information, but I had a more immediate question to resolve. "Do you think I should try to talk to the tree or something when we get there, so the Silver Goddesses will help us with our journey?"

Ken stared at me. "You should not, under any circumstances, get anywhere near the Sacred Silver Tree, Yui. The Silver Goddesses grant their blessings to the faithful. What might they do if they found you?"

"Oh."

He probably had a point.

HOW TO DEFEAT A DEMON KING IN TEN EASY STEPS

We advanced into the next room slowly, searching for traps. We didn't see any. The large room ahead had a gap in the center, leading down to a pool of water far below. There was a single broken pillar in the center of the room, perhaps one that had served as support for the ceiling in the days when the temple was aboveground. Across the room was a single switch, and a door next to said switch.

I ignored the gap and the switch entirely, grabbing Ken.

"Blink."

We teleported across the room to the door. "Ph—"

Ken pushed the door open before I could finish my Phase spell. It was unlocked.

"You don't always have to use magic on everything."

I shrugged. "But I like to."

We walked into the next room, or rather hall. It led to a single shaft that descended down a long distance. I couldn't even see the bottom.

"Inventory. Remove rope and grapple." I handed one side of the rope to Ken, and he lowered me down toward the waterline. As soon as I got close enough, I reached down to touch the water.

Then I concentrated my mind.

Inventory. Add water.

I drained the entire passageway as Ken gradually lowered me downward. I got a little wet in the process, since I had to reach into the water each time I wanted to activate my Inventory, but it was worth all the effort to avoid having to go completely underwater.

There were two areas where we could have stopped.

About ten feet down, the shaft opened up into a large chamber with no doors, but a single obvious crack in the wall on one side—another wall we were supposed to break open with explosives.

I ignored it for now. There was room to descend farther through a gap in the floor, so I kept moving down.

Another twenty feet or so down the shaft, I neared the ground. I could see a tunnel that led farther ahead, but as I drained the water, I saw something else on the ground—a single brick.

I landed on the ground, eyeing the brick. Then, with a shrug, I reached for it.

Gigantic spikes protruded from the sides in an instant, and huge eyes opened on the top of it.

I screamed. I am not ashamed.

Ken yanked upward, pulling me toward the room above, just as the now-spiked brick began to roll toward me.

The spiky brick crashed into the wall behind where I'd been a moment before, and Ken pulled me all the way up with surprising ease.

"What happened?" he asked.

"Spikey brick!" I managed, still calming from my panic.

"Spikey . . . brick . . ." He frowned. "Oh! You must mean a brick mimic!"

"There are brick mimics?" I stared. Suddenly, the entire world seemed like a more hostile place. Ordinary mimics were bad enough. Why did brick mimics have to exist?

Ken nodded gravely. "They're very dangerous. You're lucky one didn't hit you—I think they're well above our level. Hold on."

We headed down to the room one level below us, with just the crack in the wall. Then, I lowered Ken with some difficulty toward the floor.

"Scan," he said, testing out the newest spell he'd learned. He'd gotten it when he'd gained a level at the same time I'd unlocked the Bard class. "It's Level 30, and it has a weakness to fire magic. Pull me back up."

Level 30 was pretty scary. As far as I knew, levels for monsters generally only went up to around 50, and those were the inhabitants of the Demon King's Castle. The absolute limit on class levels was supposedly 99, but I wasn't aware of anyone—human or monster—that had ever actually reached it. We didn't have good records of the levels of Heroes and Demon Kings, but most people agreed that they were probably in the 60 range.

I grunted, pulling him back up as requested. "That's a bit over our level, but I think we can handle it. We don't have fire magic, but maybe we can just avoid getting hit. I could shoot some arrows from up here?"

"No, Yui. It can climb. You're lucky it hasn't already. It probably just didn't see you as a threat, but it will if you attack."

I paled. "Uh . . . okay. Are there traditional methods for handling brick mimics?"

"Yes, of course." Ken nodded. "But we're not going to use them."

I blinked. "What?"

"I have a better idea. How much did you say your Inventory could store?"

A few minutes later, we returned to the top of the shaft.

A single, seemingly innocent brick lay at the bottom of it. Waiting. Watching.

If we tried to fight the brick directly, there was a good chance it would obliterate us. Ken was right—we were desperately under leveled for this place.

But, as it turned out, there were some things that were more important than levels.

"Inventory." I put my hand over the shaft. "Remove pillar."

A fifteen-foot-tall granite pillar appeared in front of my outstretched hand. It fell immediately.

I couldn't actually see the brick's eyes open, comically wide, as the pillar fell down the shaft with a satisfying crunch. But I did imagine that as I saw the message that appeared a moment later.

[Your party has killed a brick mimic.
You have gained 4,517 experience points.]

Ken and I burst into delighted laughter, giving each other a fist bump of approval.

I hadn't expected Ken to suggest that I steal the broken pillar from the temple's entrance. That seemed pretty atypical for him, but I couldn't complain. It was a nice trick, even if it did reduce the building's already questionable level of structural stability a bit further.

Defeating the brick mimic was a ludicrous amount of experience for such a small effort. I almost wanted to go find more brick mimics, if they didn't absolutely horrify me.

We climbed down the shaft after that, and I touched the top of the pillar. The bottom had been damaged a bit in the fall, but not a lot.

"Inventory. Add pillar."

The pillar vanished.

We proceeded to the bottom of the pit, then continued cautiously

HOW TO DEFEAT A DEMON KING IN TEN EASY STEPS

down the hall. If the brick mimic had been Level 30, that meant anything else here was very likely to be in the same range. We couldn't hope to defeat most monsters of that level in a straight fight.

The thin pathway led straight into a much broader chamber, one that had been filled with water until I drained it.

It was a huge circular room, one that looked to take up a good portion of the interior of the temple. There were three floors visible, each with multiple doors on either side.

A runic pattern on the floor near where we entered looked familiar, and I suspected it was one of the switches meant to raise and lower the water level. (I had, in fact, caught that part when Ken had been telling me about it—I just had more fun things to focus on at the time.) We ignored it, instead focusing on the dozen horrific monsters that stared at us as we entered.

The monsters were terrifying, gigantic fish, with skull-like heads that were fixed in permanently horrifying expressions. Their eyes glowed with red light, and their wide jaws snapped open to reveal huge fangs.

"Scan." Ken frowned. "Level 31, weak against lightning magic. They'd normally be very dangerous."

I gave him a nod. I agreed that normally, they would have been a terrible threat. They were, however, currently flapping helplessly on the now-dry temple floor.

Even raising and lowering the water level probably wasn't meant to drain this room entirely. At the moment, we had a pretty easy solution to the fish, regardless of how tough they were.

"Inventory. Remove pillar."

Crunch.

[Your party has killed a skullfish.
You have gained 4,185 experience points.]

It only took a minute to walk around the room and smash them all.

[You have gained a level.]

It turns out that fighting Level 30-something monsters at Level 15 is a good way to level up quickly, if you can survive the process.

I put the level into Bag Mage. That got me one new spell, Flicker, which would briefly make me incorporeal just before, say, a swordsman could cut me in half. The spell would then wear off immediately, but it worked regardless of how strong the attacker was. It was a super-powerful defensive tool, but unfortunately, it also had a huge mana cost. I wouldn't be able to use it more than a few times in a row without resting.

Ken put his level into Sword Saint and learned the Moderate Strength spell, which was a direct upgrade for his old Lesser Strength.

After clearing the monsters, we inspected the rest of the room. It didn't take long to find what I was looking for—a single door on the bottom floor that was much larger and more intimidating than the rest, with a gigantic keyhole.

The door to the boss room.

There were still at least eight other rooms in the temple to explore, and likely more. There was almost certainly something to be found behind the mysterious crack in the wall in the room we'd already passed.

But after seeing the level of the monsters inside this temple, I realized we'd been tremendously lucky to find the ones thus far in situations where they'd been easy to attack without any chance of reprisal.

If we walked into a room with a few brick mimics surrounding us, or even just a chamber with a few more conventional Level 30-odd monsters... I didn't like our odds of surviving that.

The Water Temple Hero had failed here somehow, in spite of his power. I didn't know how, but that meant there was a good chance that we'd run into something unfair or unexpected if we tried to search the whole place.

So, I took a look at Ken and gestured toward the giant door. "You ready?"

Ken looked at me, no longer showing his usual skepticism. "Just a moment." He walked over, putting a hand on my shoulder. "Moderate Strength. Protect. Bless. Bless Weapon."

Then he took a breath and repeated the process, casting the same spells on himself.

"Flicker." I cast my new spell on myself, then on him. I immediately felt drained, the tremendous mana cost of the spell hitting me with a wave of fatigue. I shook it off as quickly as I could. The beneficial spells we'd just cast wouldn't last long enough for us to rest and recover our mana.

With that, I put my hand on Ken's shoulder. "Phase."

We stepped through the giant door, and I knew immediately that I'd made a terrible mistake.

The moment I stepped into the room, I found myself elsewhere. I mean, I guess that's obvious, but I mean I wasn't in some kind of obvious stone chamber inside a temple.

No, we seemed to be in some kind of forest. I could see the sun shining brightly in the sky above us, grass beneath us, and a wall of trees surrounding the entire area.

I mean that last part in a very literal sense; the trees were clustered together so tightly that they formed a solid barrier, with tremendous roots and branches blocking any hope of passage beyond.

I briefly wondered if I could Phase through them, but it wasn't an immediate concern. There were a couple more eye-catching things to worry about.

First, there was a stone doorway on the opposite side, maybe a hundred yards away from us. It was just sort of... sitting there, with no walls around it. Presumably, there was magic stuff going on with that. I assumed we were supposed to defeat whatever horrible monster was lurking nearby before going through.

Even more important, there was a gigantic tree right in the middle of the area. It was the largest tree I'd ever seen, larger even than the dead tree that had served as the entrance to our first dungeon. It had bright silvery bark, and the leaves that hung from branches high above us glittered like silver.

The last of the Sacred Silver Trees.

I wasn't a particularly faithful person, but even I had to admit it was an awe-inspiring sight. I found myself walking toward it and subconsciously reaching out with a hand.

"Yui, wait!" Ken grabbed me by the shoulder.

I blinked, surprised both by Ken's gesture and my own incaution.

"We're not alone here," Ken whispered.

I saw him then, barely visible. A man seemingly formed of living shadows, resting his back against the surface of the colossal tree. He had a harmonica pressed against his lips, but no sound emerged from it.

He wore an archer's cap, a tunic, and a single-edged sword at his side. A kite shield was strapped across his back, and a bag of equipment sat on his belt. A bow and quiver of arrows sat nearby.

While both he and his equipment looked to be made of solid darkness, I thought I could just barely catch a hint of color on his clothing. A shadow of what might have once been green.

"The Hero's Shadow," Ken hissed. "A challenge designed to match the Hero against someone with his own abilities. He's intended to be the last challenge before confronting the Demon King."

I narrowed my eyes. My grip on my sword tightened.

We'd come a long way. I knew we'd be facing deadly challenges. But someone with the same abilities as a legendary Hero . . . that was something I'd been utterly unprepared for.

Nevertheless, I couldn't give up. I gave Ken a nod, then marched forward, sword in hand.

The Hero's Shadow didn't move. He just waited right against that tree, watching us. Watching me.

Ken hesitated, then moved forward to walk alongside me.

As we drew closer, I noticed something else. Beneath the Hero's Shadow was a stone circle inscribed with magical runes, similar to the type I'd seen in the temple holding the Hero's Sword. It was the only stone in the whole place—the rest of the ground was all dirt and grass. It looked similar to one of the pillars we'd seen outside, but with only the top portion exposed.

I assumed they had something to do with the tree's connection to the goddesses, but I couldn't be sure. Perhaps it was simply another one of the ways we could raise or lower the water level in the temple, similar to the pillar we'd found outside.

"Hero's Shadow!" I called out as I approached. "I am Yui Shaw, and I intend to fight the Demon King. Will you let me pass?"

The Hero's Shadow lowered his harmonica, putting it into the bag at his side. Beyond that, he made no other movements.

Ken raised his sword into a defensive stance. "I believe we need to challenge him to proceed."

"I'd really rather not. Let's just walk around?"

Ken sighed. "If you insist."

We kept our distance from the tree. The Hero's Shadow turned to watch us, but he made no move to follow.

Eventually, we reached the door on the other side of the tree. I shoved at it, but it didn't budge.

"Phase." I stepped forward.

The door flashed. A blast of energy hurled me backward. It stung a bit, but it didn't cause much real harm. More important, bright runes began to appear all along the surface of the door.

The skies above us darkened, bathing the entire forest clearing in a twilight glow.

As I recovered from the shock from the door, I heard the sound of a creak behind me.

I spun, but not fast enough.

The Hero's Shadow was right behind me, a blade of solid shadow already raised to strike.

"Yui!" Ken hurled himself in between us, his own sword flickering upward.

The shadow's sword flickered to the side, his arm movement so fast I couldn't even follow it. When his blade met Ken's, I felt a tremendous burst of pressure in the air. Then Ken shot backward, hurled with impossible force by the simple act of meeting the shadow's blade. Ken smashed into one of the trees that walled us into the area with an audible crack.

I let out a yelp, then charged forward while the Hero's Shadow still had his blade out of position.

That was a mistake. The Hero's Shadow shifted into a stance that mirrored my own exactly, meeting my strike with an identical strike of his own.

Identical, save for the force involved.

I had both Moderate Strength and Bless spells active. My physical strength and durability were significantly enhanced. But when my sword met his, the sheer power of his motion bent my wrist back almost to the point of breaking. I fell backward in sudden agony, dropping my sword entirely.

If he'd chosen to lunge just then, he could have ended me in an instant.

He didn't. He simply stood and watched, maintaining the same combat stance I had used a moment before.

I wasn't going to take any risks that he'd change his mind. I stepped on my sword, shoved it into my Inventory with a mental command, and then spoke. "Blink."

The spell teleported me backward to Ken's position along the forest wall.

The moment I appeared, I reached down and grabbed him. "Blink." I teleported both of us as far from the Hero's Shadow as possible, all the way to the opposite side of the area, where we'd first entered.

I hoped that it would give us a moment to breathe.

By the time we finished teleporting, the Hero's Shadow was standing in front of me. My eyes widened in shock.

The Hero's Shadow unslung his shield from his shoulder for the first time, moving it in front of him into a defensive stance. Then he tapped the pommel of his sword against it in a gesture with a clear meaning.

Come and get me.

"Moderate Heal." A warm light washed over me as Ken spoke, and the pain of my injuries subsided. Ken had split the spell between us, affording a bit of healing to us both.

I tilted my head down.

"Inventory. Remove sword."

My sword reappeared in my left hand, and I raised it into a defensive stance. Ken rose unsteadily to his feet, then raised his own sword.

The Hero's Shadow continued to watch silently, but his own eyes narrowed in focus. I thought I saw a hint of something familiar in them.

Determination, perhaps.

"We strike together," Ken said. "If he continues mirroring us, perhaps one of us can hit within the moment he reacts."

I nodded.

"Three...two...one."

We struck.

"Holy Slash!" Ken brought his sword down in a two-handed sweep, the sword's edge glimmering with sacred light.

HOW TO DEFEAT A DEMON KING IN TEN EASY STEPS

The Hero's Shadow brought his own sword down in an identical motion, a swirling mass of shadows collecting around it.

"Blink."

While their swords met in a blast of divine power meeting darkness, I appeared behind the Hero's Shadow and jabbed my sword at his back.

It was a beautiful combination move, if I had to say so.

But we'd struck moments apart. And that heartbeat of delay between our attacks was more than enough.

The Hero's Shadow battered Ken's attack aside easily, driving Ken's sword into the ground, and then swung around and met my thrust with one of his own.

My sword collided with his. This time, his motion didn't jar the sword out of my hand—it blasted my blade straight out of the way, pushing toward my heart.

I Phased out of existence the moment the sword passed into my chest. My Flicker spell had just barely saved my life.

I stumbled backward, reeling. The Hero's Shadow pulled his sword back, returning to a ready stance.

Ken came in swinging again, but when the Hero's Shadow moved his blade in the way, Ken made his real move. Releasing his grip with one hand, Ken pulled something out of his robes and hurled it at the Hero's Shadow.

With a powerful-enough healing item or spell, you even destroy certain types of undead outright.

The potion bottle hit the Hero's Shadow straight in the chest, drenching him in liquid.

A heartbeat passed, then the Hero's Shadow turned his head

down, wiped at the liquid and glass on his chest with his shield, and shook his head at Ken.

He hadn't been hurt in the slightest. But now, for the first time, he was moving without provocation.

With a single motion, he ran Ken through.

Ken staggered backward, staring at the sword in his chest in disbelief... and then realized that he, too, was still unharmed. The sword had passed right through him.

I'd used the Flicker spell on him, too.

And while the Hero's Shadow was distracted, I took the window I'd been given. I commanded my Inventory with my mind.

Remove five units of water.

A jet of thousands of gallons of water blasted out of my free hand, released with incredible force. It was so wide that I couldn't really control it, but I didn't need perfect aim.

The Hero's Shadow spun, raising his shield. Yet in spite of the tremendous pressure of the water, he wasn't pushed back a single inch.

While he blocked the water with his shield, his sword moved to block a series of rapid strikes from Ken. His blocks came with incredible speed, requiring him to shift his sword to flick Ken's out of the way at seemingly impossible angles.

I pushed more and more water out of my Inventory, but eventually, the Shadow simply vanished.

When he reappeared right in front of me, I was ready.

Inventory. Remove pillar.

The Hero's Shadow lunged at me just as a pillar dropped from the sky above him.

He aborted his lunge mid-movement, jumping and flipping over, his sword making a circular blur.

The tremendous pillar split apart in midair. First in halves, then with each half falling apart into a dozen smaller slices.

The Hero's Shadow landed on his feet a moment later, already in a defensive posture.

I stared blankly at him.

That's... not even fair.

The Hero's Shadow banged his shield with the pommel of his sword again. A challenge. It made no sound.

My own growl in response did, though.

"Blink." I reappeared behind him.

Inventory. Remove spiked block.

"Blink."

I repeated the process, then blinked away again.

Two spiked blocks surged inward toward the Hero's Shadow, moving of their own accord.

I dropped a third from above him.

His motions were a blur, too fast for me to see.

When the blur of shadows ended, the blocks were gone, and only a pile of rubble remained.

During that time, though, I'd pulled something else out of my Inventory.

I couldn't hope to hit the Hero's Shadow directly; he was simply too fast. But I didn't have to hit him directly—he was standing in a puddle. I'd drenched the whole area with thousands of gallons of water, after all.

I pointed the Lightning Rod at his feet. The Hero's Shadow

started to move almost immediately, but for once, he was too late. The rubble pile had walled him in.

"Volt."

At my command, a blast of lightning shot from the rod, electrifying the water—and the Shadow within.

A burst of smoke rose from where lightning met the Shadow's body...

...And as the smoke cleared, he stepped right through it.

Entirely unharmed.

The Hero's Shadow vanished in a blur of sudden movement. I didn't see him again until after I felt the snap of the Lightning Rod being cut in half.

Ken struck at the Hero's Shadow again from behind, only to have his assault deflected with ease. Ken went flying backward, and I retreated as quickly as I could.

The Hero's Shadow watched.

"Blink."

I appeared next to Ken, grabbing him, and then cast Blink again.

I didn't take us far. Just a dozen feet or so away, enough to give us a moment to breathe. "Healing?" I asked.

"Moderate Heal," Ken whispered, pressing a hand against me. My right arm, nearly incapacitated by my first parry, felt a little better. I switched hands, then concentrated.

"Inventory. Remove shortsword."

My old shortsword appeared in my left hand. With two weapons, I hoped I could keep up with the Hero's Shadow a little better.

The Hero's Shadow didn't reappear next to us this time. He simply advanced toward us, casually, retaining a defensive posture.

HOW TO DEFEAT A DEMON KING IN TEN EASY STEPS

"Flicker." I cast the spell on Ken, feeling an intense drain of mana. I couldn't afford the cost to cast it on myself again after that, but I didn't regret using it on Ken first. As the healer, he was our higher priority. "What are his weaknesses?"

"Scan," Ken whispered. His eyes widened. "No..."

"No? He has no weaknesses?"

The Hero's Shadow continued to advance toward us. Twenty feet away, then fifteen.

"It's worse than that. He has no weaknesses, but... Yui, you need to leave. Now."

I frowned. "Why? I think we can—"

Ten feet away.

"Two... hundred and fifty-six."

I raised an eyebrow at Ken. "What?"

"His level, Yui. It's two hundred and fifty-six."

The Hero's Shadow stopped in front of us, just barely out of swinging reach.

And as my expression shifted from determination to one of utter horror, the Hero's Shadow smiled.

"Yui, go!"

Ken launched himself forward, swinging faster than I'd thought possible. Once again, his blade ignited with holy light, this time seeming to shine brighter than ever before. It was as if it was burning with his resolve, his determination.

The Hero's Shadow smashed his attack out of the way with a casual swipe, then blurred forward and smashed at Ken with his shield.

The Flicker spell stopped that from hitting Ken, but the Hero's

Shadow didn't stop. The spell faded as Ken moved backward and the Hero's Shadow stepped on Ken's boot. With Ken in place, the Hero's Shadow buried the pommel of his sword in Ken's chest.

Ken doubled over. Another strike from the Hero's Shadow hit him straight on the back, driving him to the ground.

"Ken!" I screamed, launching myself forward and hurling my shortsword with my left hand. It was a desperation move, but as I'd hoped, the Hero's Shadow shifted for just an instant to knock the sword out of the way.

That was enough. I put my hand on Ken's back and dragged him toward me. "Town Gate!"

Escaping a fight was my last resort, but Ken was right—we were outmatched by an unfathomable margin. We had no hope of defeating an opponent like this.

And so, I put all my hopes into my last spell—and nothing happened. No portal appeared to greet us. There was only silence, and the weight of the knowledge that I had failed.

A split second later, the Hero's Shadow had slashed Ken across the chest.

Ken hit the ground face down, unmoving. I screamed, but my scream didn't last long.

A sword of shadow sliced my throat open in the next instant.

I hit the ground, falling to my knees. My remaining sword fell from unfeeling fingers. My vision blurred with tears.

... Why ... why did it have to end like this?

The Hero's Shadow raised his sword, preparing to end my life with a final strike.

And then I heard the sound of breaking glass.

HOW TO DEFEAT A DEMON KING IN TEN EASY STEPS

"STOP!"

Someone was in front of me, then. A tiny figure, her arms stretched out to serve as a barrier between my life and my demise.

The Hero's Shadow froze mid-swing.

And, as I watched in awe, his arm began to tremble.

Vex glowered up at him, her tiny form burning with anger. "You... I can't believe you." She balled her hands into fists. "Don't you dare move."

Then Vex turned toward me, floating closer, and kissed me on the cheek. I felt warmth spreading through me, and the wound on my neck immediately began to close.

Vex floated to the ground, landing next to where Ken was lying in a pool of gathering blood, and kissed him on the back of the head. I saw a brief glow. I didn't know if what she was doing would be enough, but he began to stir on the ground.

Then, Vex flew upward toward the Hero's Shadow, seemingly undaunted by the terrible threat he presented.

And, as I watched in awe, she slapped him in the face. "You... can't take them from me!" Tears streamed from her eyes. "I won't lose my Hero again!"

The eyes of the Hero's Shadow widened. The sword of shadow fell from his limp grasp, and he raised a hand up to his face where she'd struck him.

Then, silently, he lowered his head.

Vex flew lower, lifting his chin and forcing him to look at her. "How could you? How could you leave me alone like that? Do you know how long I waited for you?"

And then I understood.

The Hero's Shadow stared at her with sad eyes, then shook his head. His sword hand reached up toward her, but she slapped it away. He frowned.

Ken barely pushed himself from the ground, still clutching at his chest. He looked at where his sword had fallen nearby, but I shook my head at him.

He frowned, but nodded.

The Hero's Shadow continued to focus on Vex. She gritted her teeth, then flicked him in the forehead. "You're going to let them through here, you understand? They're finishing what you started."

The Hero's Shadow dropped his shield, then raised his hands and made a series of signs I couldn't understand.

Vex sighed, then moved her hands through a series of similar motions.

I glanced to Ken.

"He says he can't. Something about...bound?"

I raised an eyebrow at that.

Tears continued to stream from Vex's eyes. "You...you can't be like this. I don't understand. I...you...I thought you died, you know." She sucked in a ragged breath. "I thought I..."

The Hero's Shadow reached for her again. This time, she let his hand wrap around her, bringing her to his chest.

"Why is she...?" Ken turned to me.

"He's the Water Temple Hero," I said, confident now. "The Hero's Shadow is the Water Temple Hero. The one who failed."

"No," Vex said, her tiny voice barely audible. "Not failed. He never failed. He was punished."

"Punished?" Ken asked. "But why?"

HOW TO DEFEAT A DEMON KING IN TEN EASY STEPS

The Hero's Shadow turned his head toward the tree, then made a swift, cutting gesture. Then he released Vex from his grip. As she floated away, he made a series of more complex signs toward her.

Ken gasped. "No. It's not possible."

"What's he saying?" I asked.

"The Demon King didn't burn down the other Sacred Silver Trees."

I blinked. "What? Then—"

The answer was apparent, but Ken answered for me regardless. "He did."

"But... why?" I asked.

Vex turned toward us, wiping tears from her eyes. "To end it. The cycle."

I turned my head toward the last gigantic tree. "Then these..."

Vex nodded. "These trees are the path between the world and the heavens. And they are what ensures the continuing reincarnation of the Hero... and the Demon King."

My eyes narrowed toward the gigantic tree. "What happened?"

"I traveled with the Hero to the other dungeons, just as any faerie would," Vex explained. "And we cleared them in record time and with ease. He was the strongest of all Heroes—not purely out of natural talent, but because of his determination to reach his goal. The end of all Demon Kings, forever. And as we searched for clues, we discovered the true nature of the Sacred Silver Trees. Their power is what maintains the cycle of reincarnation. Without them, neither Heroes nor Demon Kings will return to the world."

My mouth opened and closed, but no sound emerged.

Vex continued. "When he discovered this, he was furious. The goddesses themselves were maintaining the cycle that destroyed the world, time and time again. He sought to stop it—and he almost succeeded. As he approached the last tree, he knew that the goddesses would seek revenge against him for his audacity. And so, he sent me away and entered this place alone."

Vex lowered her head. "I stood outside, waiting for him, my heart filled with hope. And then I watched as the earth trembled, and the island carrying the Water Temple descended into the lake below. I tried to swim down to make my way into the temple, but it was sealed."

She drew in another deep breath. "I waited for him. For a hundred years, I waited. But he never returned. It was only with the coming of the next Hero that I . . . accepted it. That he was never coming back."

The Hero's Shadow lowered his head, closing his eyes.

"Then . . . what's this? What is he? What's he doing here?" I gestured at the Hero's Shadow.

The Shadow made a few more hand signs.

"Cursed," Vex explained. "Eternally cursed. For attempting to destroy the trees, the goddesses cursed him. The seal beneath the tree forces him to guard it, protecting the tree from harm, and preventing any but the next Hero from reaching the room where the next key is held. In this, he ensures that the cycle remains."

"But . . . why? Why would the goddesses want the cycle to continue indefinitely?" Ken shook, his eyes turning skyward.

"Even we never discovered that." Vex shook her head. "But he believed that the cost in lives could not possibly be worth it, whatever their goals were. So, he rebelled. And for that"—she looked at the Hero's Shadow—"he was punished."

"How can we help?" I asked.

The Hero's Shadow looked at up at me, an expression of surprise on his face. Then, slowly, he shook his head. He made a few more signs toward Vex.

"He says he cannot allow you to harm the tree, or to advance into the next chamber. If you sought to finish what he started, he would have to stop you. Such is the purpose of the curse."

I frowned at that. "And the seal that keeps him bound is . . ."

And then, for the first time, I realized we might have a chance.

"Walk with me for a moment."

We walked—well, Vex floated—toward the colossal tree.

The Hero's Shadow watched me cautiously.

"Don't worry, I'm not going to attack the tree. Can you tell me if the goddesses are watching us now?"

He made some signs. Vex translated. "He does not believe they are watching directly at this moment, but they would respond in an instant if the tree is harmed. They trust that he would handle any invaders, however, and rarely bother to watch this place otherwise."

Ken glanced at me. "We can't possibly cut down the tree before they'd notice, even if he somehow could stop himself from protecting it."

"We're not going to do anything with the tree. That'd be suicidal. But the tree isn't the only thing here. Hero's Shadow, you only have to guard the tree and the door. Is that correct?"

The Hero's Shadow gave me a dubious look, but nodded.

"Good." I smirked. "Inventory. Remove pickaxe."

A pickaxe appeared in my right hand.

The Hero's Shadow raised a spectral eyebrow.

"Ken, got enough mana left for a Moderate Strength spell? Mine is wearing off."

"Sure, but why?"

"Because this is going to go a lot faster with one."

Ken frowned, putting a hand on my shoulder. "Moderate Strength."

I nodded to him. Then, I got to work.

Ten minutes later, I'd managed to break through a square section of tile enough to separate it from the rest of the ground.

This was, of course, the section of tile that held the curse binding the Hero's Shadow to the area near the tree.

"Are you ready to try this?" I asked him.

The Hero's Shadow retrieved his sword and shield, offering me a salute. Then, after sheathing his sword, he made a sign at Vex.

She gasped, then trembled in place, lowering her head. Tears once again freely flowed from her eyes.

I didn't ask Ken what the Hero had said. It didn't seem like it was my place to ask.

Then, the Hero's Shadow turned to me and nodded.

I knelt to the ground and pressed a hand against the glowing ritual area. "Inventory."

```
[Your Bag Magic has successfully overcome
     this object's Magic Resistance.]
```

The tile vanished, ritual circle and all.

The Hero's Shadow reached out for Vex one last time—

Then vanished into nothingness.

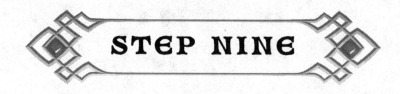

PREPARE FOR THE FINAL BATTLE

THERE WAS A MOMENT of silence as the Hero's Shadow vanished. Then Vex burst into bawling and buried herself in my chest.

I lowered a hand to quietly brush her hair as she cried. We waited like that for some time.

"Thanks, Vex. You saved us."

She looked up, her eyes still filled with tears. "I . . . did?"

I brushed her tears away with a finger. "You did."

Vex cried a little more quietly for a while after that.

Finally, when the tears ceased, it was time to move on.

With the Hero's Shadow gone, the mysterious door ahead of us was open. We stepped within to find a stone room with a platform leading up to a treasure box. Within it, we found a glimmering golden ring.

I stabbed both the box and the Pentacrest Piece. Neither was a mimic.

We took the Pentacrest Piece. And with it, we headed back to town.

We rested easy for the next few days. We both needed it. That fight had brought us both to the brink of death, and some recovery felt necessary.

During that time, my mind was still whirling with plans. I mapped out the next few places we should visit. We debated going back to the

Water Temple to clear it out for any further treasures held within, but after seeing how deadly the monsters were, we felt it would be smarter to find someplace closer to our own level range to focus on.

Before any of that, though, I decided to pay one last visit to home.

My parents were so immensely, beautifully proud of me. I hugged them tight, with the knowledge that I might not return.

From there, I made my way to the place we'd truly started our journey.

"Is it... really necessary to sneak in at night?" Ken asked.

I gave him an apologetic look. "For what I'm planning? Absolutely."

"Am I going to regret helping you with this?"

I gave him a shrug. "Do you regret helping me so far?"

"I'm undecided."

I snorted. "Fair enough. Well, you can decide on how you feel when this is all over, then. I'll be curious."

"I will be, too." He sighed. "Very well, I will help you."

"Good. Just get the door open and wait outside. If this works, I won't be long."

"You don't want me in there?" He sounded surprised, and maybe a little wounded.

I pressed the two pieces of the Pentacrest we'd earned into his hands. "No. Because if this fails catastrophically, I want you to finish this without me."

"Yui... I... no. I can't."

I gave him a hard look. "You can and you will. People are counting on us to do this, Ken. Don't forget that."

He gave me a grunt of agreement. "I won't."

"Good. Now, let me get in there."

"You really won't tell me what you're going to do in there?"

I shook my head. "No. Sorry, Ken. You'd try to stop me if you knew."

"That's... not really reassuring."

"I know." I smiled at him. "But trust me, okay? I think there's at least a two-in-ten chance this works. And if it does, it'll be a real help."

"And the other eight in ten?"

I winced. "Well... it's been really nice, Ken. Our adventure."

Ken sighed. "Go on. Let's see this through."

I nodded.

As planned, I didn't tell Ken what I was going to do in the Sword Shrine.

I won't tell you either. Not just yet.

But I will tell you what I told him when I walked out of the temple, only minutes after I entered.

"It worked." I burst into laughter. "It actually worked."

"Yui... what worked? What have you done? Did you manage to pull out the sword?"

I laughed again. "Not, uh, exactly. We have to go."

"Go? Why? Yui?"

"I'll, uh, tell you later. For now... we have three more temples to beat. Preferably before anyone takes too good of a look inside the shrine."

With my secret business at the Sword Shrine completed, it was time to get back to clearing the remaining temples.

I considered our remaining options: Fire, Earth, and Metal. In the sequence, the Fire Temple was supposed to be the second one we visited, and Water was last.

Now that we'd completed one temple out of sequence, I hoped that would be enough to throw off any of the Demon King's forces that were hunting us. Given that we'd been able to handle the Water Temple, going to the Fire Temple seemed like it would be easy, as long as we weren't intercepted along the way.

We bought more basic supplies. Healing potions, antidote herbs, that sort of thing. I bought some mana potions this time, too, since running out of mana was a real risk now that I had the Flicker spell. I suspected that having an Inventory still filled with hundreds of thousands of gallons of water would make the Fire Temple a lot easier than it would have been under ordinary circumstances.

I was feeling optimistic. It took a few days to make the trek to the Fire Temple, and we even took a few minor side jobs along the way, earning coin and gaining one more level. We both chose to advance our main classes.

That brought me up to Level 14 in Bag Mage, and Ken up to Level 14 in Sword Saint. I got a single new spell, Lesser Teleport.

Lesser Teleport was similar to Blink, but with a much longer teleportation range. I could send people close to half a mile, which was pretty useful. It also could carry a larger number of people—up to six, as long as we were in physical contact.

More important, it also didn't require me to have a line of sight to the destination. That meant I could use Lesser Teleport to teleport to other rooms inside a dungeon, for example, or even teleport out of a dungeon entirely if the entrance was nearby.

The main disadvantage was the mana cost. Even with my Cheapskate skill, I'd have to use Lesser Teleport sparingly.

Ken got one called Magic Barrier, which specifically focused on protecting against offensive magic.

It was upon arriving at the Fire Temple that I realized I'd made a very serious miscalculation.

That was because, unfortunately, there was no Fire Temple.

Where the legendary structure had once stood, I found only a tremendous crater.

For a time, Ken and I simply stared at it. "Could . . . it be somewhere else?" I lifted the map of the area. "The map is a little unclear."

"I . . . think he . . . destroyed it." Ken trembled. "He destroyed one of the Five Temples."

"Shouldn't that be . . . ?"

"Impossible," Ken finished for me. "Just as impossible as an ordinary person working through the Five Temples to defeat the Demon King."

It was easy to forget that this Demon King had progressed further, faster than any in recorded history.

It was easy to forget that I was not the only person in the world with agency. I was not the only person who could try new things, to defy tradition. To change the formula by which the world had operated for centuries.

I'd been caught completely off guard.

Without the Pentacrest, was defeating the Demon King even possible?

I spun to Ken. "We... have to search the ruins. Find any trace of the Pentacrest."

Ken nodded swiftly. We moved into the crater, sweeping the area. With Moderate Strength spells and the ability to shove huge rocks in my Inventory, we swept through the rubble for hours and hours. We even let Vex out of her bottle to help.

Of the Pentacrest Piece, we could find no sign.

"Could we make a new piece?" I asked Ken.

He turned his gaze downward. "It took much of the power of the Silver Goddesses to create the Pentacrest. A mortal making a replacement... it's unthinkable."

"Then we'll have to get it back from the Demon King. He has to have it."

Ken winced. "A Demon King wielding even one fraction of the Pentacrest's power... his strength will be unfathomable."

"Can they even be used on their own?"

"Yes, but only by a Hero or Demon King. Without the Hero class, our own pieces are largely useless except as a key to bypass the barrier in front of the Demon King's fortress. They should still have worked for that—if we had all five."

I sucked in a breath. "We'll have to make do with four, then."

"Or beg the goddesses for aid. Perhaps they could..." Ken trailed off, but I understood his thinking. Perhaps divine providence would aid us when hope seemed lost.

But I had no interest in begging for goddesses to solve our problems. Given what had happened to the Water Temple Hero, I was feeling more and more like they were the ones that created our problem in the first place.

I didn't say that to Ken. He was clearly having some doubts of his own, but he was still a man of faith. I respected that too much to push him further. He'd come to his conclusions on his own, or ask me if he wanted my opinion.

We were united on one thing, at least. We needed the remaining pieces as quickly as possible.

We pushed ourselves to exhaustion each day. We ceased doing any additional side jobs as we trekked across the continent, making our way to the Earth Temple. I used Dimensional Magic liberally to expedite our travel. It didn't accomplish much—I didn't have any long-range travel spells aside from Town Gate, and that couldn't get us anywhere new.

Still, every moment felt necessary. We were in a race now, one with terrible consequences if we failed.

And so, it was with that knowledge in mind that we reached the Earth Temple—

And found that it, too, had been completely obliterated.

Four days later, we found the crater where the Metal Temple had been. Once again, there was no sign of the Pentacrest Piece that had once belonged in the temple.

Instead, we found something else. Or rather, someone else.

A tall man with dark blue hair sat among the rubble, an open book laying on his lap. A tremendous two-handed sword rested sheathed on his back, a black gemstone set in the pommel that seemed to drink in the light itself. He wore huge, thick spectacles and long robes that matched the color of his hair. Over the robes, he wore mismatched bits of black armor.

I wasn't an expert on armor, but I was pretty sure the exposed portion on the lower part of his chest was a pretty serious flaw in his armor's design, and the big spikes on his shoulders were going to be a problem if he had to go through any doorways.

He had thick bandages wrapped around his right hand, and I thought I could see something red glowing beneath them. Perhaps a cursed injury, or some sort of hidden magical item.

He looked up, startled, as I approached. His swift movement in standing dislodged the book from his lap, and he fumbled with it for a moment before it fell to the ground. He grimaced, looked up at us, and stammered, "H-hullo there."

I approached slowly, raising empty hands. Ken hung back, an odd expression on his face, like he wasn't quite sure what he was looking at. I spoke as I came closer. "It's okay, we don't mean you any harm."

The blue-haired man gave a nervous smile. "I— I, uh, know. I've been waiting for you, you see. You're, uh, the Hero?"

I gave him a smile. "I wouldn't call myself that, but some people seem to, and I intend to give it a good try." I offered him my hand. "I'm Yui."

"Y-Yui." He gave a strained look at my hand, then cautiously reached out, as if my hand was going to bite him. He grabbed the edge of my fingers and shook them up and down briefly before darting back, like he'd never shaken a hand before. "I'm, uh. Dirk. D-Dirk Lord."

"It's nice to meet you, Dirk." I glanced around the area. "If you don't mind me asking, why were you waiting for me?"

"I, uh, you see . . ." He raised his hand behind his head, looking embarrassed. "I was hoping, maybe, I could join you? If it isn't too much trouble."

I raised an eyebrow. "You want to join me? To confront the Demon King?"

He nodded. "I, uh, think it's very important. And, maybe I could help a little? If you'd have me, that is."

"What classes do you have?" Ken asked.

Dirk's head spun, his eyes widening slightly as if seeing Ken for the first time. With a trembling hand, Dirk reached up to adjust his glasses. "Um, uh, just one, sorry. It's, uh, Dark Lo—erm, I mean, Dark Knight. Dark Knight is, uh, what I meant to say, is the name of my class."

Ken gave him a serious look. "Dark Knight is a very rare class, but quite powerful. You get a mixture of weapon skills and offensive magic, yes?"

Dirk looked from side to side, then back to Ken. "Y-yes. I can do both of those things."

Ken looked to me. "We could use an offensive magic wielder. It's one of the few things we're really lacking."

"We could use more offense in general, really," I replied. "I'm much more utility focused, and your powers lend themselves more toward healing and defense." I turned toward Dirk. "I think you might be a good fit for us, Dirk."

His expression brightened immediately. "R-really?! I'd be ever so grateful!"

He seemed so genuine and excited, it was hard not to like him. But I did have a few reservations. "Listen, Dirk. I'm not going to lie to you. Our quest is very dangerous, and there's a good chance we're going to fail. And if we fail, we're very likely going to die."

For once, Dirk didn't stammer in his response. He seemed to straighten a little, too. "We're all going to die anyway if we do nothing."

"You might be right. But there are other options. You could wait it out for a new Hero to arrive, like in the old times. Or you could travel to another land, like some people are."

"Or trust in the goddesses to provide for us," Ken added. "They have never failed to intercede in our times of greatest need."

Dirk's expression hardened. "Goddesses. Indeed." He shook his head. "I think I'll take my chances with you, uh, Yui. And . . ." He turned toward Ken.

"Ken. Ken Sei." Ken smiled, finally walking closer. "Before we take you somewhere dangerous, I'd like to see some of your skills. Would you be willing to fight a monster for us? We could help if you need it."

"A . . . m-monster?" Dirk asked. "Like a dragon?"

Ken laughed. "There's no need to start with something that big. We could go hunt something smaller, like goblins, or something else novices start with."

"Or slimes," I suggested. "We could fight—"

"Anything other than slimes," Ken interrupted. "We will not be fighting any more slimes. Ever."

His tone brooked no argument.

Dirk shook his head. "N . . . no. That's not why I suggested a . . .

I didn't mean..." He looked pained, clearly having trouble finding the words. "Hold on."

He winced, turned, and fled off toward a cavern entrance on the side of the mountain where the Metal Temple had once stood.

We waited and watched for a time. Minutes passed. Ken asked, "Should we go... get him or something?"

I hesitated. "Maybe. I'm getting a little worried. If he isn't back in a few—"

And then I saw him. I froze.

He walked slowly toward us, dragging something heavy behind him. "S... sorry..."

He lifted and dropped it in front of us.

"I, uh, mentioned the dragon because, you see..."

I looked at what he'd dropped in front of us. It was, unmistakably, the top half of the body of a dragon.

"I, uh, kind of already killed one."

STEP TEN

DEFEAT THE DEMON KING

FOUR ADVENTURERS MADE THEIR way to the Demon King's Castle.

Well, three adventurers and a faerie. I'm still unclear if Vex counted as a party member or not, but let's give her the benefit of the doubt.

The Demon King's Castle was located on the farthest edges of the dark continent to the west. Traveling there took weeks. As we progressed across the continent, we dodged assassins and fought terrible monsters. The journey was difficult, but in the end, we stood proud at our destination.

The castle was surrounded by a dome-shaped barrier of dark energy. According to legend, the only way to pierce it was through the full power of the Pentacrest.

We were about to put that to the test.

The first test was the simplest.

I threw a rock at the barrier. It disintegrated on contact.

Next, I walked closer.

Ken put a hand on my shoulder. "I don't really think this is a good idea."

I glanced back at him. "Do we have better options?"

He winced. "Not really."

"I— I could, uh, b-blast it, for us?" Dirk offered.

I shook my head at Dirk. "We can try that, but the odds that you have the power to overcome the Demon King's barrier are pretty low." I'd seen Dirk in combat over the last couple weeks of travel, and while his abilities were admittedly impressive, I didn't think he'd be able to overcome the barrier with brute force.

I still didn't know exactly how powerful Dirk was. He was weirdly cagey about the subject, but I put that down to social awkwardness and embarrassment. Ken had tried to cast Scan on Dirk once or twice, but it didn't work properly for some reason. He presumed it was because of some kind of Dark Knight class ability.

"I—if you say so." Dirk frowned, clearly wanting to say more.

"We'll keep it in mind as an option. For now, I'd prefer to try things that are a little less direct. So, let's get started, shall we?"

Thus, we began Operation: Dig a Giant Hole.

My Inventory skill was useful for storing huge amounts of water. I'd wondered if, perhaps, I could store huge amounts of ordinary dirt and stone instead. This seemed like the perfect time to test it.

I touched the ground and concentrated my mind.

But when I tried to Inventory the ground, I got just a single grain of dirt. I sighed. Apparently, the earth beneath us was considered multiple "items," whereas units of water weren't. I didn't understand the reason it worked that way, but it meant no instantly digging tens of thousands of pounds of earth into my Inventory.

With that approach failing, we tried it the hard way.

"Inventory: Remove Shovels."

Ken groaned. His hand glowed as he reached for one. "Bless Weapon." Then, he touched each of us. "Moderate Strength."

Blessed shovels, weirdly, were more effective than normal ones. We dug pretty fast.

Unfortunately, we found just what we'd feared—the barrier wasn't just a dome. It was a sphere. We dug a solid ten feet down to confirm, but we saw no sign that the barrier abated farther underground.

"What's next?" Ken asked.

"I'm thinking I try to Phase through."

Ken shook his head vehemently. "Good odds you explode, doing that."

"Fair, but Blink is probably going to do the same."

"That just means they're both bad ideas, Yui."

I groaned. "Fine. Let's try this. Phase." I Phased myself out while holding a rock. Then, I tried to hurl the still-Phased rock through the barrier.

The rock exploded.

I was glad I hadn't tried to Phase through the barrier.

"Okay, next." I picked up another rock. "Blink." I didn't cast the spell on myself—I tried to Blink the rock itself across the barrier to the other side.

The rock vanished. Then there was a brief flash in the air.

No rock appeared on the other side of the barrier.

I stared at the empty space where the rock should have been. "Hm. I'm going to call that a draw."

Ken stared daggers at me.

I stared right back. "Well, Ken, if you're going to be all judgy like that, it's your turn."

Ken gulped. "I...suppose it's for the best this way." With great hesitation, he removed the Pentacrest Pieces from his bag. He approached the barrier, raising the two glowing rings, one with each hand. "Silver

Goddess, hear my prayer. I beseech you, aid us in this time of desperate need, and clear our way toward this final confrontation."

The golden rings flashed brightly...

And then, as one, we saw a message flash in our vision.

[Insufficient Pentacrest Pieces.]

We groaned. The bright glow around the pieces faded, subsiding to their normal, milder level.

Ken shook his head. "We've breached tradition to this point, but it seems we've reached our limit."

"Not just yet." I shook my head, turning toward Dirk. "Okay, your turn. Explode the wall."

"Wait, wait, let's at least back up first?" Ken pleaded.

We backed away. Ken cast Magic Barrier on us.

Dirk stared at the wall as if it was his deadliest opponent. Then, he raised his right hand. Carefully, he began to unwrap the bandages. "For this... I'll need to use a fraction of my true power."

I was impressed. I'd never seen him take off the bandages or look quite so serious.

A brilliant red glow enveloped his outstretched hand, growing stronger by the second. The skies darkened, the clouds turning black. In the distance, I heard thunder, and a palpable wave of pressure manifested in the air around him. The earth beneath us trembled and quaked, slowly beginning to break apart.

Lightning struck from the skies, surging toward Dirk's hand, then collecting around it. Static energy hissed in the air.

My eyes widened—I'd never seen such a potent display of magical power gathering, from Dirk or otherwise.

Then with an expression of great focus, Dirk said, "Demon King Obliteration Beam."

I was amazed that apparently he had a spell meant specifically for defeating the Demon King—that showed great foresight. Perhaps he'd suffered some sort of tragic loss at the Demon King's hands, and this was his way of seeking revenge.

The blast that ripped forth from his hand was colossal, with the raw kinetic energy released blasting Ken and me backward and toward the ground.

A tremendous beam of crimson light shot out toward the barrier—then the world went white.

The next thing I remember was the ringing in my ears. I couldn't see, not right away. Then I felt the ache, all over my body.

My eyes opened, but slowly. I was on the ground.

It was a good thing Ken had told us to back away, because as I examined the area from my position on the ground, I realized I was just at the edge of a titanic crater.

The entire area just in front of the barrier had been obliterated. It looked almost like the scene of what had happened to the last three temples, which definitely wasn't suspicious in any way.

I pushed myself upward with a groan. Ken and Dirk were on the ground nearby, similarly disoriented, but largely unhurt. Ken's Magical Barrier spell and foresight had saved us.

We took a moment to regroup. Ken treated our minor scrapes and bruises with healing spells.

And then we looked at the barrier—or rather, what remained of it.

The barrier was still in place, but flickering violently. In fact, there were moments here and there where it briefly failed entirely, only to reappear in place a second later.

Dirk hadn't managed to break the barrier, but he'd done something incredible—he'd damaged it. Enough, perhaps, that we could make our way through.

We exchanged looks. For once, Ken didn't argue. "Good work, Dirk."

Dirk blushed furiously. "I, uh, thanks, I guess." He busily began to rewrap the bandages around his right hand. I thought he might have some sort of glowing crest on it, but I didn't get a good look at it. "It's nothing." He turned away.

"You feeling ready to go in?" I asked.

"We'll have to time it carefully," Ken responded.

We exchanged nods, then cast a round of beneficial spells. Flicker, Moderate Strength, Bless, all that stuff.

We chugged mana potions. We needed to be in our absolute best shape if we were going to confront the Demon King.

Then, it was finally time. We all joined hands. We'd do this together, or not at all.

We waited for one of the moments when the barrier appeared to vanish, then I spoke. "Lesser Teleport."

And together, we were inside the barrier.

We headed to the castle's front doors. They swung wide open as we approached.

The Demon King, it seemed, was expecting us.

The entrance to the Demon King's Castle was a long hallway lined with red carpet. Weapons and armor hung on the walls, as well as the same kind of magic torches that I'd seen on the walls of the Wood and Water Temples.

I approached one of the weapons and put a hand on it. It was affixed to the wall, but that sort of thing didn't stop me.

Inventory.

> [Your Bag Magic has successfully overcome this object's Magic Resistance.]

A sword vanished into my bag. I had no idea if it was purely decorative or not, but I wasn't going to pass up potential demon castle loot.

"Yui. Focus," Ken said, his tone insistent.

"Fine, fine." I led the way down the hallway.

We reached a pair of double doors. There were no signs of traps or monsters, which seemed a little odd, but perhaps the Demon King knew that ordinary monsters and traps would serve little purpose against us.

I shoved the doors open. They led into a wide-open chamber.

A colossal monster awaited us within. He was nearly seven feet tall, with the upper half of a man in golden armor and the lower half of a snake. His six muscular arms each carried a huge curved sword.

We entered the room, bracing for battle.

"Welcome, Hero . . . to your end!" The muscular half serpent struck a dramatic pose, twisting strangely and flexing each arm. I was both impressed and slightly confused.

"Is that . . . ?" I whispered, half to myself.

Ken shook his head, apparently having heard me. "No, not the Demon King. I think that's . . ."

"Behold, mortals!" the serpentine man interrupted. "I am the Master of Muscles, the Sovereign of Swolleness. I am Mighty Mordragon, the First of the Four Demon Generals!"

"Ooooh, that explains it." I'd known that each Demon King would have four generals, but they were different every time, so I hadn't recognized him on sight. "So, we have to fight you to pass, I take it?"

"Mmm!" He nodded furiously. "You may try. But surely, you will lose!"

Dirk looked at us, his expression bleak. And slowly, he reached for the bandages on his right hand. "You . . . must press on, Yui. I will hold him here."

"Uh, Dirk. Why? We could, you know, just fight him as a team."

"No . . . that's not how this is done." Dirk looked strangely determined. "You, the Hero, must move on. Your companions must fight the Demon King's Generals to buy you time for your final battle."

"Yeah, but no. That approach makes zero sense. We could obviously just—"

Ken interrupted me. "He's right, Yui. This is our destiny. Though you may have your way of doing things, don't deny us our roles. We have come this far, and if we choose to play out the roles companions are meant to play, you must allow us to do so."

I let out a deep, heavy sigh. "That's . . ." I was about to argue again, but I saw Dirk's and Ken's expressions.

All this time, I'd done things my way. Chosen the path for our whole group without regard to the desires of the others. But if my companions wished to play a role in the story in their own way, what right did I have to deny them that?

I gave Dirk a firm nod. "Good luck."

Ken leaned over, giving Dirk a quick hug. "I will pray for your success."

Dirk froze, startled by the sudden show of affection. "T-thanks. I'll... uh... fight him now. Go on."

Ken and Dirk broke apart.

"I won't let you leave!" The Master of Muscles jumped forward, descending from the skies and swinging all six blades in our direction.

Dirk hurled himself in the way. "I will be your opponent." His greatsword slipped free from the scabbard on his back, and in a series of incredible movements, he parried all six blades with the single sword of his own. "Go!" Dirk yelled to us, never taking his eyes off his opponent.

We ran. Behind us, I was aware of the sound of steel clashing against steel. I heard Dirk say the words to some kind of incantation, then I felt a blaze of heat behind us.

Then Dirk began to cackle, and I heard a grunt. I couldn't tell who had made it.

I was on the other side of the room then, pushing the doors open into the next hall.

Together, Ken and I ran forward down the next hallway, identical to the last.

I didn't stop to loot swords this time. I couldn't justify it, not while Dirk was fighting so hard to buy us the time needed to reach the Demon King.

We came to the next door. And, just as before, it opened into a wide chamber.

Within it stood—or rather, floated—a man in black robes. I say "man," but really, I couldn't determine a gender, or even if the person was a person at all. Within his robes was no face, merely a void of darkness.

"Humans," the void's voice echoed across the room. "I am the Deacon of Darkness, the Bishop of Blackness—Darkpitch Blacksoul, the second of the Demon King's Generals. And I will obliterate you here!"

Ken stepped forward, his sword already outstretched to his side. "Holy Sword." His blade glowed with inner light, and he turned to me. "This is where I leave you, Yui."

"Ken . . . thank you. For everything."

He shook his head. "Don't thank me. But before you go, these belong to you." He reached into his bag, handing me the two golden rings.

I slid them into my Inventory with a nod. "Take care, Ken."

"I will. You too. And when I've beaten this opponent"—he turned toward the Bishop of Blackness—"I'll see you again."

"Hah!" the Demon General laughed. "Don't joke, fool. You've seen your final dawn."

"We'll see." Ken rushed forward.

So did I, but not on the same path. I ran straight past him to the next door.

And then, for the first time I could remember, Ken was no longer by my side.

I ran and ran. There might have been something wet in my eyes.

Then, I burst into the next room.

A woman hovered in the center. She had beautiful, long black hair, and she wore all dark garb. Shadowy energy emitted from her hands.

The only things about her that weren't dark were the beautiful butterfly-like wings on her back.

"Come here alone, have you?" She smiled at me, revealing sharp, vicious fangs. "Then you've come to fail. For I, the Pernicious Pixie, the Fallen Faerie, Fatal Flower will defeat you!"

I heard a pop from within the bag at my side, and a familiar, tiny voice rang out through the air. "She's not alone, idiot!"

"You." The Fallen Faerie spat venom. I mean that literally; there was poison dripping from her mouth as she spoke. "The Faerie Who Failed."

Vex floated in front of me, balling tiny fists. "No. Not anymore. After today"—she glowed with a bright light—"I'll be the Faerie Who Defeated You."

"That's . . . kind of a vague title," the Fallen Faerie replied. "But you'll never claim it either way! Die!"

The faeries flew at each other.

I rushed down the hall, now familiar with the routine.

And then I reached the next room.

It was, so far as I could tell, completely empty.

The door slammed shut behind me.

I was standing in utter darkness, and I knew there was a serious problem.

I was alone.

And there's one critical thing about the Four Generals of the Demon King—

There are four of them.

And I'd run out of companions to sacrifi— I mean, um, leave behind to bravely confront my opponents.

I was on my own against an unknown opponent, with no one to buy time for me to proceed toward my goal.

With a moment of concentration, I removed a magic torch stolen from the Wood Temple's walls from my Inventory. It bathed the room in light, but little else.

"You...dare...bring...foul...light...into...my...domain...?"

The voice seemed to echo all around me.

"Uh, yeah. Kind of need it to see." I searched the room but failed to find my opponent. The low light of the torch illuminated dark stone, but showed no monster. I thought I caught hints of movement out of the corner of my gaze a couple times, but I couldn't follow it.

I had very few means of directly attacking someone. I kept my torch in one hand and a sword in the other, hoping they would be enough.

"I...am...the Viceroy of Void...the Deacon of Darkness..."

I paused. "Wait, wasn't Darkpitch Blacksoul the Deacon of Darkness?"

There was a moment of silence.

"Wait...hold on..."

I heard some shuffling.

"No...that...one...is...definitely...me..." the voice hissed. "...He...got...confused...again..." I heard a sound of a sigh. "...It's...really...quite...infuriating...when...he...takes...my...titles..."

I nodded in sympathy. "Well, maybe you should go, uh, fight him for it?"

"...Maybe...later..." the voice rasped. "...After...I'm...done...killing...you!"

I braced for an attack, but it came from behind me, and too fast to counter.

Huge claws grabbed for my spine, ready to sever it in a single swipe.

I would have been torn apart if not for the hurled knives that embedded themselves in the claw before it could reach me.

I heard a hiss from behind me, startled, and then the creature retreated back into the dark.

And then they appeared in a burst of smoke next to me, their dark garb allowing them to blend easily into the shadows of the room.

The legendary ninja who was very definitely not the missing Princess Fitzgerald. Nameless Kage.

"You... came to rescue me!" I gasped.

"No." The ninja shook their head. "I came to defeat the Demon King. But"—they smiled—"this opponent is in my way." The ninja gestured toward the door. "Go. I will defeat this foe."

I gave Nameless Kage one final nod, then rushed toward the door.

I heard the clashing of metal and claws behind me, too fast for me to follow.

And then I burst through the door, into the next hall, and finally to the last chamber in the castle.

The throne room.

The doors slammed shut behind me, but that didn't matter.

I was far past the point of turning back.

The chamber was a huge circle, the floor made from some kind of black reflective crystal.

Upon an elevated dais stood a throne. In front of it was a pedestal, upon which sat three golden rings.

The last three pieces of the Pentacrest, very nearly within my reach.

But as close as they were, I couldn't focus on them. My eyes focused on the Demon King, my enemy, my lifelong enemy. He sat on the throne, a great black sword draped across his knees, and smiled at me.

"Hello, Yui," the Demon King said. "I've been expecting you."

I knew his words to be true. Not just because he'd opened the door for us, or because of how he'd destroyed three temples to claim the rings on the pedestal in front of him.

No, he'd known because he'd been with me.

The man sitting on the throne was none other than Dirk Lord.

I was shocked by this unexpected and completely unpredictable twist. "D . . . Dirk? But why?"

Dirk laughed, standing from his throne and jamming his sword into the floor. "Why? Why did I join your party and lead you here, bringing the last two pieces of the Pentacrest straight to me? Why did I leave the path clear, save for Demon Generals to separate you from your few pitiful companions?"

"No." I shook my head. "I understand all that. I . . . just want to know . . . if you're really the Demon King . . . why did you pick a terrible name like Dirk Lord?"

The Demon King snarled, vanishing and appearing right in front of me. "That is my actual, perfectly acceptable name!"

I blinked. "Oh, sorry. I didn't mean to offend you."

"No matter!" he shouted, a little bit too loud. He brought up his tremendous sword. "You have proven a worthy opponent, Yui, but you have foiled my plans for the last time. I will defeat you, and then nothing will stand in my way!"

"Except the Silver Goddesses," I pointed out. "And, of course, the Hero, when he returns to defeat you."

Dirk snarled. "It doesn't matter. I've taken precautions. Once I have the entire Pentacrest, none shall stand against me!"

"Really?" I asked. "You don't think the goddesses that created the Pentacrest and started your entire cycle of reincarnation have the ability to do anything else? They couldn't, say, take away your powers, or deny your ability to use the Pentacrest?"

Dirk snorted. "I fear not the goddesses. They, too, will someday feel my wrath."

I nodded appraisingly. "Good, good. I was thinking the same thing."

The Demon King stared at me.

I stared right back at him.

There was a moment of awkward silence, then he said, "Wait, hold on, what?"

I gave him a wry grin. "Dirk. You don't really think I didn't realize who you were, did you? With a name like that?" I shook my head. "I admit, the stuttering was adorable acting. It's a cute touch."

"I . . . uh, acting, yes. That is, uh, precisely what I was doing." The Demon King flushed. "But wait, what was that you were saying before?"

"Right. The goddesses." I sheathed my sword. "For centuries, the Silver Goddesses have perpetuated a cycle of violence between humanity and demons. I've studied the war extensively, and I realize that you, much like the Heroes of yore, have simply been fighting to protect your own people from the endless conflicts that have struck time and time again. Each time you rise, you conquer more territory for your people. Each time the Hero does, your people are slaughtered, and dismayed, you are driven back to the afterlife. This time"—I waved toward the Pentacrest Pieces—"you sought to end the cycle, using the same power the Hero uses to defeat you. It's clever. But it'll never work. I went into the restricted archives in the Sacred Shrine, and I discovered something important. Two Demon Kings have gained the entire Pentacrest before. Both were transformed into horrible monsters, only to be defeated by the Hero as soon as he revived."

"I will be different," Dirk hissed. "I will not be beaten so easily. I will find a way to subvert the power of the Pentacrest for myself."

I gave him a shrug. "Maybe. Or maybe the Pentacrest is just one more trap laid by the goddesses. Maybe you're compelled to seek it out, only to be doomed to failure."

Dirk snarled. "Then I will destroy you, and the pieces as well!"

"Won't work." I shook my head. "The Dearly Departed Demon King tried it."

"Gaah!" He balled his fists. "Then what would you have me do, Yui Shaw? Give up? Allow the Hero to defeat me? I will not permit it!"

"No," I said, shifting the golden rings to my other hand. "I have a better plan."

I reached out with my right hand, offering it to him. "Join me, Demon King, and I will allow you to rule half the world."

He looked at my hand, then back up to me. "That's... kind of supposed to be what I'm supposed to offer the Hero."

I nodded. "I know."

"And he always refuses," Dirk pointed out.

"I know." I smiled. "But, in case you haven't noticed . . . I'm not very heroic, am I?"

"No," the Demon King admitted. "You are something far, far worse."

I raised an eyebrow. "Oh?"

"You're clever. The kind of clever that comes with a deep arrogance. It makes you believe you're capable of anything." Dirk turned his head upward and laughed. "It makes me almost want to believe you."

I stepped closer. "Then will you . . ."

His head snapped downward, his eyes glowing. "Yui Shaw . . ." A blazing aura ripped forward from his body, the heat of it pushing me back. ". . . If you can defeat me . . . then, and only then, I will consider your offer."

I gave him an uneasy nod. "Very well, Demon King." Then, a wry grin stretched across my face. "Let's dance."

The Demon King struck in an instant, faster than I could hope to match. His speed, power, and skill were all greater than my own.

His blade passed straight through me. My Flicker spell was still in effect.

But it could only save me once.

Blink.

I vanished, reappearing right next to the pedestal carrying the three golden rings. Then, still carrying the other two, I reached down and touched them together.

The five rings were joined as one.

I won the fight in a single move.

. . . Hah! Just kidding, it obviously wouldn't be that simple.

When I clicked the rings together, nothing happened, save for a strange, non-metallic sound.

The Demon King moved, faster than I could see, and appeared right in front of me.

I stared incredulously at the rings on the pedestal. He waited as I reached down and touched one. "Are these . . ." I peeled back some of the golden foil on one of the three rings. ". . . Chocolate?"

The Demon King smiled. "You're not the only clever one here, Yui Shaw."

And then he hit me.

He hit me so hard that I flew backward, smashing into the throne. I felt something in me crack, and then a surge of pain like nothing I had ever experienced.

If he'd used his sword, rather than a bare hand, I had no doubt he would have split me in half.

My vision turned red for just an instant on impact, and by the time it cleared, he was standing in front of me again, sword raised. "You didn't think I'd put the real pieces in plain sight like that, did you? Come now, Yui. I'm not the kind of Demon King that makes things so simple."

"I know." I coughed. "That's why I like you."

"L . . . like?"

Blink.

I vanished again, crossing the room. Not to the entrance, but to a corner. I needed to buy time to think.

He spun. I drank a healing potion and recast my Flicker spell.

I knew I had no chance in a fair fight against the Demon King, but a fair fight had never been the plan.

HOW TO DEFEAT A DEMON KING IN TEN EASY STEPS

Inventory. Remove ten units of water.

Back at the Water Temple, Ken had asked me to put the sacred water back in the lake after we were done. It was deadly to demons and undead, being blessed with the power of the goddesses. It was why the Demon King had never breached that particular temple.

I'd neglected to put the water back. I had other plans for it.

In a matter of moments, I had flooded the Demon King's throne room with holy water.

Dirk had just a moment to shout in alarm before the water reached him, and I heard something burn.

I was submerged in the water, too, but being human, it didn't do me any harm. Well, no more than the harm of not being able to breathe properly underwater, that is.

It was possible that I should have listened to Ken when he recommended magic swimwear. I had to hope the water would burn the Demon King enough to incapacitate him before I drowned.

As I watched Dirk through water-blurred vision, however, I realized that I had significantly underestimated him.

The burning I'd heard wasn't Dirk's skin exposed to holy water. It was the sound of his blistering hot aura obliterating the water before it even came close.

And so, as I briefly floated in the water, I saw a very angry Demon King walking slowly toward me, completely unhindered by the small lake that I'd dropped into his throne room.

He raised his right hand, and it began to glow.

Crud.

I did not like the idea of being hit with a Demon King Obliteration Beam.

Blink.

I moved again, a wave of exhaustion hitting me as I reappeared behind the throne and took cover.

A moment later, there was a colossal explosion. The room trembled, and much of the water within it evaporated in an instant. Fortunately, that same water—and a surprisingly sturdy throne—served to dampen the blast to the point where it barely hurt me.

With a thought, I drained the rest of the water in the room, then grabbed and drank another healing potion.

A moment later, Dirk's sword flashed straight through the throne, cutting it in half and very nearly bisecting me. My Flicker spell triggered again.

Exhausted, I took a swing at him. He parried easily, but that was fine.

I stepped in while our swords met and put a hand on his chest.

Lesser Teleport.

I didn't cast it on me. My Blink spell, of course, could be used on other people—and Lesser Teleport had much better range.

I teleported Dirk straight out of the room—and directly into the obliterating barrier field that surrounded his castle.

For a moment, I was alone.

I did a quick search, finding a false wall in the most obvious place possible—right behind the throne. With luck, perhaps it would lead to where the last of the Pentacrest Pieces were located.

I couldn't find the switch to open the false wall, but I didn't need one. I was just about to Phase straight through the wall when Dirk reappeared in the center of the room.

His body was smoking, and his clothes badly burned. He glared

HOW TO DEFEAT A DEMON KING IN TEN EASY STEPS

at me. "You . . ." His fists tightened, and he trembled. "You actually hurt me."

I beamed at him. "Ready to surrender and join me, Demon King?"

"I am far from beaten!" He raised his sword, the blade blazing with blackness. "Enough of this! I will end you with my next strike!"

The world around him trembled. I could feel the entire castle shaking, and I heard sounds of something snapping as glimmering lines appeared next to him with every passing moment.

. . . Were those cracks appearing in the air? Yeah, that was definitely not something that should happen.

I renewed my Flicker spell again, but I knew it would not be enough to handle an attack of that magnitude.

No, for this, it was time to deploy my final, most desperate plan.

I couldn't possibly beat the Demon King. I'd known that from the start.

But there was someone who could.

Only a True Hero could wield the Hero's Sword and defeat the Demon King. And, as it so happened, I had one available.

Inventory. Remove Sacred Platform.

A ring of stone appeared on the ground in front of me. A glimmering circle of binding force that had once stood in the Water Temple, near the Sacred Tree.

And along with it appeared the Hero's Shadow, bound to the location of the platform for defying the will of the Silver Goddesses.

In his right hand, he held a shield formed of solid shadow.

And in his left, shining with unsurpassed brilliance, was the Hero's Sword.

I had never found a way to take the Hero's Sword out of the shrine on my own, you see. My spells were never strong enough to defeat the enchantments the goddesses had placed on the platform. But ultimately, I hadn't needed to.

All it required was a True Hero to draw and wield the sword. And the Water Temple Hero—the man who had become the Hero's Shadow—was the most powerful Hero who had ever lived.

I'd known the Hero's Shadow had been tied to the location of the sacred platform that had trapped him in the Water Temple. I'd taken the platform out inside the Sacred Shrine, allowing the Hero's Shadow to appear and draw the sword. Then, I'd stored the platform again, causing the Hero and sword to be stored inside my Inventory along with it. Then, I'd used my Project skill to create an illusion of the Hero's Sword in place of the real one. It wouldn't trick people for long, but I'd gotten away without anyone noticing.

After all that, I'd kept the platform in my Inventory until the perfect moment.

Now, the battle between the Hero and the Demon King could finally begin.

STEP ELEVEN

THERE WERE ONLY TEN STEPS, WHAT WENT WRONG?

THE HERO'S SHADOW SURGED across the room, his blade a flash of silver in the dark.

Dirk, to his credit, reacted in an instant. He brought his own blade down so quickly that I couldn't even follow it.

I chugged mana potions as I watched the show, just in case.

The Hero's Shadow blocked with his shield, then riposted.

And, for the first time, Dirk Lord—the Demon King—began to bleed.

Staggering backward, Dirk reached a hand to his chest in disbelief. "You..." he hissed. "I will destroy you!"

The Hero's Shadow didn't respond with words. The Hero, I'd been told, had always been the silent type.

Instead, he bashed his sword and shield together. The message was the same as when he'd made that gesture against me in the Water Temple.

Come and get me.

The Demon King was happy to oblige, but perhaps not in the way the Hero had hoped. He flickered and vanished, reappearing right behind the Hero's Shadow, already swinging a crippling downward cut.

It was a mistake.

After all, Spin Attack was the Hero's signature move.

In a single motion, the Hero's Shadow spun, leaving a trail of silver in the air as he slashed across Dirk's chest. Dirk fell backward again, then vanished, appearing across the room. "Let's see how you like this! Burn in the fires of the abyss, Hero!"

With an outstretched hand, he hurled a sphere of energy in the Hero's direction.

The Hero's Shadow brought up his sword and, with casual ease, smashed it into the energy ball—sending it straight back at Dirk. The Hero's Sword could reflect magic, after all.

The energy ball hit with crippling force, and Dirk shuddered at the impact.

The Hero charged, and Dirk recovered to meet him.

Their blades sang, exchanging blows with lightning-fast speed and incredible skill. For a moment, they appeared evenly matched.

But Dirk, for all his power and cunning, was a Demon King. He was at an inherent disadvantage against the Hero, the one opponent he could never truly defeat in an equal contest. And this Hero was the strongest one who had ever lived.

Slowly but with great certainty, the Demon King was losing the battle. It was clear from his expression that he knew this, but he did not withdraw.

At first, I thought this was mere stubbornness on his part. Perhaps he thought that, with a lucky strike, he could upend fate and defeat the Hero himself.

But I had, once again, underestimated the Demon King.

And I'd forgotten that, like me, he was not alone.

As the swordsmen exchanged blows, Dirk switched to a one-handed grip on his sword and feigned a lunge. The Hero took the opening immediately and struck Dirk, his sword plunging deep into the Demon King's chest.

HOW TO DEFEAT A DEMON KING IN TEN EASY STEPS

Dirk dropped his sword, grabbing the Hero's blade with one hand. And with the other hand, he snapped his fingers. "Goodnight, Hero."

Mighty Mordragon, the first of the Demon Generals, appeared right behind the Hero. And, as Mordragon brought six swords down at once, the Hero's Sword remained trapped in the Demon King's chest.

Blink.

I appeared back to back with the Hero's Shadow, deflecting two of the descending swords. Two hissed past me, missing. One whooshed through me, nullified by my Flicker spell.

But the last of the six swords hit me in the right shoulder, cutting deep. I screamed in agony, then kicked Mighty Mordragon in the chest.

He didn't even budge.

The Hero did, though. With a sudden surge of strength, he ripped his sword free from Dirk's chest.

Dirk coughed, falling back, and then vanished, reappearing near the throne.

I stumbled, too, falling gracelessly to the floor.

The Hero jumped in front of me, his single sword deflecting a rain of incoming strikes from the Demon General.

I Blinked again, out of the way of the fight, and pulled another healing potion out of my Inventory. While I drank it, I watched as Dirk began to glow brighter and brighter, his crimson aura spreading farther with every passing moment.

Dirk burst into laughter, then a fit of coughing. After a moment, he wiped blood from his lips and spoke. "F...fools...you...think...you've won? Just because...you've...injured me...and...defeated my generals?"

Mighty Mordragon looked wounded. "Hey, boss, I'm still right here—"

The Hero's Shadow slammed his shield into Mordragon's face, and the Demon General fell unconscious to the floor.

Dirk cackled again, clapping his hands together. An enervating wave flowed across the chamber, and I felt my strength fade as it struck me. I fell to the ground, barely able to move.

The Hero's Shadow didn't seem affected in the slightest. He strode toward the stairs to the throne with great confidence, his sword still blazing with light.

Dirk staggered forward to the pedestal in front of the throne, and in that moment, I realized I had made a crucial mistake.

...I might have kind of left my Pentacrest Pieces on top of it, next to the fake chocolate ones.

"Blink," I said in a panic, as Dirk pulled out the necklace that was tucked into his armor, revealing three golden rings attached to the chain.

[You have insufficient mana to use this spell.]

The wave of enervating magic that had crossed the room had drained almost all of my mana. I didn't have enough left to Blink.

I reached out with my right hand. "Gravity." The rings twitched but didn't fly toward me. They were too far away.

I opened my Inventory and began to drink a mana potion, but I wasn't quick enough.

Dirk tore free his necklace, pressing his three rings on top of the two that were already on the pedestal.

And with that, the Pentacrest was whole.

HOW TO DEFEAT A DEMON KING IN TEN EASY STEPS

The Hero's Shadow lunged, faster than I had ever seen anyone move.

He still wasn't fast enough.

The whole world stopped.

All except for the Demon King, who held the completed Pentacrest in his hands. With a great laugh, he raised it above his head.

"Silver Goddesses, I have claimed your power for my own!" Light spread across his body, tremendous energy flooding into him. He cackled... and then bent over double. "This is... No... What is... happening..."

Dirk broke into coughing, then gestured toward me.

I felt something then. A trembling in the air, and I was freed from the effect that had held me in place.

I sighed, shaking my head. "I warned you."

Wings burst from Dirk's back. Horns shot out from his head. His hands shifted into vicious claws. A spiked tail descended from his spine.

Dirk trembled, falling to the floor. "What... is... this..."

"That," I explained as I barely pushed myself to my feet, "is your second form."

The Pentacrest slipped free from his grasp, tumbling to the ground.

And Dirk, still growing and shifting into a more bestial state, howled into the air.

The Hero's Shadow might have struck then—but he remained frozen in place, as if time had stopped for him.

Whatever power that had activated when the Pentacrest had been touched still held him, and I had no idea how long it would last.

It was up to me to end the nightmare.

Dirk turned toward me, his eyes blazing with pain and rage. "You...you did this. You tricked me!"

I shook my head sadly. "I didn't want it to end this way. I still don't want it to. We can end this together, if you'll let me."

"No...no..." He held his hands to his head, as if to block out a sound only he could hear. "I can't. I can't! Agh!" He screamed again. "I need more power. More power! With it, I'll change everything!"

He picked up the Pentacrest and lifted it again over his head. It began to glow, brighter than ever before.

Power began to build around him. The strength of the Demon King and the Pentacrest combined.

I rushed toward him, only to be rebuffed by the sheer force of the power. "No, Dirk! Stop! This is insanity!"

He paid me no heed. I tried to press forward, but I couldn't get close enough to reach him.

The energy began to build, the air around him crackling dangerously. The throne room trembled, rocks falling from the ceiling.

It was obvious what Dirk was trying to do, and it was obvious that he was going to fail. In my best guess, he had mere seconds before a detonation of power would occur, utterly obliterating everything nearby.

I couldn't possibly survive that. No one could, save perhaps the Demon King himself.

The Hero's Shadow was still frozen in place. If he could have moved, perhaps he would have been strong enough to shield us somehow. Perhaps with the reflective power of the sword.

...The sword.

A plan clicked into my mind just in time.

"Blink." I appeared next to Mordragon's unconscious body and grabbed him. With my Unencumbered skill, I was able to carry him easily.

"Blink." I appeared next to the Hero, Mordragon with me.

Energy continued to build around Dirk as he screamed. It was reaching a critical point. We only had seconds remaining before the explosion came.

I put a hand on the Hero's shoulder. "I really hope this works."

I took a deep breath.

Then I touched the blade of the Hero's Sword.

"Inventory."

I saw the flicker of a message, too fast to read, but I knew what it would say.

[Your Inventory spell has been reflected.]

I found myself floating underwater, with a broad variety of objects floating around me. Beyond the water was an endless void of darkness.

But I was not alone.

The Hero's Shadow was with me in that underwater place. He turned toward me as I reached out for him, taking my hand with his left, which was now empty.

He looked confused, but not uncomfortable. Apparently, he could breathe underwater.

I couldn't, but I'd taken a deep breath, knowing what was

likely to happen when I used my Inventory spell on the sword. I'd counted on it, in fact.

Ordinarily, there were very few things my Inventory couldn't store—people being at the top of that list. But I knew there were exceptions to that rule. I'd been able to store the Hero's Shadow by storing the platform he'd been bound to, and I also knew there was one specific case where I'd managed to get inside my own Inventory. I'd counted on doing that deliberately this time.

The Hero's Sword had, once again, reflected my Inventory spell. And now we were inside it, floating in the water that I'd stored there. Potions bumped into me in the water, and I saw a few decorative swords bobbing somewhere not far away.

Mordragon was floating nearby, too, still unconscious. I hoped he wouldn't drown right away. I was glad he'd come along with me when the spell had been reflected. I'd hoped carrying him would work, but I hadn't been certain.

I held my breath as long as I could, then sent a command with my mind.

Inventory. Remove Yui Shaw, Mordragon, and Hero's Shadow.

And then, with a moment of disorientation, I was moved again.

I landed inside a crater.

The Demon King's throne room had been utterly obliterated.

Dirk was on the ground near where the throne must have been before. He wasn't moving.

Mordragon appeared next to me. I quickly checked to make sure that he hadn't drowned, but I couldn't tell.

The Hero's Shadow appeared next to me a moment later. He immediately retrieved his sword, which was also seemingly undamaged.

The Pentacrest, however, was not.

The golden rings had been split apart, and each had been broken to pieces. The spell reflection powers of the Hero's Sword hadn't just reflected my Inventory spell—they'd reflected the Pentacrest's blast, too, straight back into the legendary object itself.

I didn't know if the Pentacrest had been permanently destroyed, but I knew I wasn't going to take any risks.

"Blink."

I teleported and immediately shoved the first broken piece into my Inventory, then rushed to collect the others. I set two in my primary Inventory, two in my second Inventory, and kept a single one physically out in the world.

I didn't want them to recombine, even by accident.

I rushed to Dirk's side. He was back in his humanoid form, his tail and wings gone.

I reached down and put a hand on his chest. I felt it rising and falling, just barely.

He was unconscious and bleeding badly, but alive.

I pulled my remaining potions out of my Inventory and used them on him. They weren't enough.

The Hero's Shadow moved. For a moment, I thought he might strike Dirk down before I could find a way to heal him. Instead, he walked somewhere else.

No, he moved to a circle on the ground, a circle of runes that had held him prisoner for millennia—now blasted apart by the Demon King's and the Pentacrest's combined power.

Only a handful of runes remained lit on the ring. The Hero's Shadow raised his sword and, with a single swift movement, sliced it apart.

The final runes flickered and died...

...And the Hero's Shadow was a shadow no more.

With a gasp, he fell to his knees.

A wave of color washed over his body. Black clothes gave way to brilliant green, and as the glow faded from his skin, I could see the ordinary brown color that shadows had concealed.

He pushed himself to his feet, lifting his arms and gawking at them. Then, with great haste, he moved to my side.

"He's dying," I told the Water Temple Hero. "Can you save him?"

The Water Temple Hero frowned, raising a hand to his chin. Then he gave a grunt and raised a finger in a "one moment" gesture.

He reached into a bag at his side and retrieved a flute. And with it, he played a melody I recognized.

The Song of Faerie Calling.

As the melody took to the air, I heard an immediate response—the fluttering of tiny wings, and then a gasp. "It's...you! It's really you!"

Vex was floating above us, gawking at the Water Temple Hero. She looked a little scraped and bruised, but otherwise, perfectly fine. "You're okay!"

The Water Temple Hero smiled at her, then made a series of quick hand gestures I couldn't understand.

"Got it. I'm on it." Vex descended from the sky, landing on the fallen Demon King's chest. Then, swiftly, she slapped him across the face.

HOW TO DEFEAT A DEMON KING IN TEN EASY STEPS

There was a spark of energy that flowed through her hand.

The Demon King's wounds sealed shut.

He burst into a fit of coughing, his eyes slowly fluttering open.

"Where... what happened?" he asked, his voice weak.

I leaned close, then bopped him on the nose. "You lost."

"I... did?" He coughed again, shaking his head. "I... must have..." His expression shifted quickly to concern, then resolve. "Then... I suppose you must take my life."

I snorted. "No, Demon King." I shook my head. "I'm going to give you half of the world."

A deal was a deal, after all.

EPILOGUE

FIND A NEW GOAL

IN THE AFTERMATH OF the battle, we found that both my companions and the Demon Generals had survived.

Ken had defeated the Bishop of Blackness in a theological trivia contest, which apparently had been sufficient to constitute an overall victory between the two. After that, he'd rushed to the next room and found the Fallen Faerie crying.

Vex had, apparently, defeated her in a contest of insulting banter. Ken, being a friendly guy, stayed with the Fallen Faerie until she felt better.

Nameless Kage and the Deacon of Darkness had chased each other around for a while, after which they'd gotten exhausted with their game of hide-and-seek and sat down to play some kind of board game instead. It was a long one, so it had still been going when the ultimate battle between good and evil was finished.

I wasn't sure if I was relieved or infuriated by how all that had played out while I'd risked my life.

Mordragon was tremendously grateful that I'd chosen to save him from the room-destroying explosion and pledged his eternal loyalty to me. I wasn't quite sure what to make of that, but he made some really impressive poses, so I decided he'd make a good ally in the future.

With the forces of the Demon King defeated (except for in the board game, which was still going), we all met to discuss the next steps.

Together, we sat in a circle in the crater that used to be the Demon King's room, and for the first time in known history, we began a dialogue between humans and demons.

"Dirk was the Demon King?!" Ken gasped.

"S-sorry, Ken." Dirk winced, giving Ken a sheepish look. "My bad?"

I sighed. The Water Temple Hero sighed with me.

Our discussions went on for much of the night.

A pact was reached.

For the time being, we would split the world between us. The Demon King's forces would peacefully fall back, allowing humans and demihumans to reclaim much of their territory, until half of the world was once again in their hands.

This was, however, a temporary measure, while we worked to implement a better one.

A better future, where humans and demons could live together in harmony. Not in different halves of the world, but together. We were more similar than different, after all.

We knew that there would be opposition.

The faithful of the Silver Goddesses would not abide any alliance with the Demon King, at least at first. We would need to work hard over time to convince them.

Ken swore to make changes throughout the church, but he knew he would face an uphill battle. His word about what had truly happened would be hard to believe for many that hadn't seen it.

Many lives had been lost among humans, demihumans, and others. Revenge would not be easily sated with words. We knew that there would be battles ahead. Not everyone would agree to peace.

But we would not be alone in our efforts in that regard, either.

HOW TO DEFEAT A DEMON KING IN TEN EASY STEPS

With a dramatic flourish, Nameless Kage removed her ninja mask, revealing that she was—to absolutely no one's surprise—actually Princess Fitzgerald, heir to the throne of her kingdom. With her powerful influence and charisma, we hoped to make changes as smoothly as possible.

As the leader of a nation, she would meet frequently with Dirk, who worked hard to reform his own Demon Kingdom toward peaceful ends. Over time, those meetings turned from professional to personal.

I suspected it might not be long before the human and Demon Kingdoms were ruled by a single family.

The Water Temple Hero, fully human once again, set off on a journey to explore the much-changed world he had awakened into. He would not be alone. Vex, having lost the Water Temple Hero once, would never leave his side again.

Together, they would travel to meet with the Great Faeries, and sway the faeries to our cause. For her great valor, Vex's title was changed; it was no longer the Faerie Who Failed. She would, forever after, be known as the Faerie Who Defeated You, just as she had boasted. This was confusing to literally everyone, but she loved it, and I adored her, so I helped spread the word.

After all that, Ken and I visited the Wood Temple again. It took significant work, but we eventually managed to move the immortal old man's entire room out of the Wood Temple and to the Sword Shrine, where he'd no longer have to live his extended life in seclusion. The old man continued to give his all-important secret to many visitors, but I don't know if anyone ever figured out what it meant.

Ken and I spent the years that followed traveling the world together. We undertook many more dangerous quests and searched for ancient treasures and secrets, growing in power and influence. We knew it was necessary to get as strong as possible for the next stage of my plan.

I might have defeated the Demon King, but the Silver Goddesses would be a much greater challenge.

AFTERWORD

MY FIRST EFFORTS AT gamelike fiction were in the days before we had terms like "LitRPG" and "GameLit." They were also spectacular failures, routinely rejected by agents and publishers alike for feeling too much like a video game. My first five books are "shelf books," which I'll never likely publish anywhere. It wasn't until my sixth book that I went the self-publishing route, testing if I could do things on my own.

At the time of writing this section, I'm working on my twenty-first book, but the republishing of this one will be my first "traditionally published" novel. That's a huge milestone to me, but this book is close to my heart containers for other reasons, too.

One of my fondest early memories is my father painting a portrait of me in a Peter Pan costume after a Peter Pan contest at a local shopping mall. (Said contest is also, very likely, my first brush with my lifelong rival slash role-play partner Mallory Reaves, but we can talk about that in another time.)

Peter Pan was my favorite character as a small child. I loved his swashbuckling style, his fearlessness, his adventures, his friendship with Tinkerbell.

AFTERWORD

But at the age of three or four, I was already taking inspiration from someone else, too.

And for that painting my father was working on, I insisted that he swap out the shorter, Peter Pan–style blade with a sword more like the one that was used by Link, the hero of *The Legend of Zelda*.

We'd only recently picked up our first game system, the original Nintendo Entertainment System. Our first cartridge was *Super Mario Bros./Duck Hunt*, and while I did enjoy pressing the zapper up against the screen in a child's first attempt at exploiting game mechanics, I wasn't really into *Mario* or *Duck Hunt*.

It wasn't until we picked up *Zelda* that I had the spark of a lifelong love.

So, I guess I should probably start this by thanking Shigeru Miyamoto, and the original *Zelda*'s design team? Maybe I should drop a line for J. M. Barrie, too. Because just as my own story starts with Peter Pan's, Link's clearly does, too. Early Link is a very clear Peter Pan analogue, though each subsequent Link would differ from him in important ways, especially in the (often wild) manga adaptations.

Zelda was different from the games that had come before. I watched my older brother play with his friends (shout-out to Aaron Rowe for letting me watch him play) for weeks or months before picking up the controller. Then, I remember just sitting down one day and playing through dungeon after dungeon, all at once. I remembered the solutions to puzzles, the path through the Lost Woods to the graveyard to get the Magic Sword (although, to my frustration, it couldn't be obtained until you had enough hearts).

AFTERWORD

The style of it—the swords and magic, the atmosphere, the puzzles—they all hooked me in a way that nothing else in my life had up to that point. That had a tremendous impact. I remember the excitement when my parents took us to the store for the holidays a year or two later—my brother wanted *Mario* 2, but I obviously wanted *Zelda* 2.

I remain a *Zelda* 2 apologist to this day, but that's another story.

Now, I could go on and on about early *Zelda* releases and their impact on me—particularly *Zelda* 3, the first title for the Super NES, and the origin of the Master Sword—or even the cartoon and Valiant Comics. But there's only so much room, so I'll thank all the people who worked on the series that inspired me so heavily, and move forward.

When the Northridge earthquake struck in January 1994, we left a badly damaged home, concerned that it might collapse entirely. I was young enough that I didn't fully process the devastation or losses, but I do remember one thing that stood out to me—

My copy of a game I'd just gotten for the holidays, *Dragon Quest* 4, had been crushed.

It sounds like such a small detail, but it was part of what made the event real for me. But that wasn't the most memorable part—

It was that my dad, seeing my reaction, patched the broken cartridge back together with duct tape. And, as if in defiance of the event, that patched-up NES game still played flawlessly.

I think the idea of that patchwork, ugly cartridge still working just fine was an important moment for me. It helped me get through the trauma of the earthquake itself, showing me there was a way to repair things and move forward.

AFTERWORD

It was also just a really fantastic game, one of the absolute best role-playing games of the era. *Dragon Quest* never had quite the US market appeal that *Final Fantasy* did—although I think they might have if they'd pushed through and finished localizing *Dragon Quest 5*—but I fell more than a little in love with that series, too. A story of Heroes, Demon Kings, and metal slimes (which are, of course, legally distinct from silver slimes).

I owe some thanks to series creator Yuji Horii and the entire design team for making *Dragon Quest* special, and to the legendary Akira Toriyama for his iconic artwork for that series and a later love of mine—*Dragon Ball*.

May Kami send you swiftly along the snake way, Toriyama-sensei.

These titles were of great inspiration to me, as were their creators, but I think it's important to note an element in all of the tales above—my family. Without the constant support of my parents, who let me spend more time than conventional wisdom may have suggested in front of a television set, and my brother, who let an annoying three- or four-year-old Andrew watch over his shoulder, I never would have reached this point in my career. They didn't buy into the anti-fantasy D&D scare of the '80s, either, and supported me when I wanted to play tabletop games, or read *Dragonlance* and the *Forgotten Realms*, which were huge impacts, too.

Now, to jump back to *Zelda* for a brief (maybe?) moment.

I loved Link, the hero of the story. I wanted to be him. I dressed up as him for Halloween.

But as time went on, I began to look at the story with a different set of eyes. And I noticed the same tropes and traditions in ever-so-many other books and games.

AFTERWORD

A Chosen One is the only one who can defeat the Dark Lord, the Demon King, the Ultimate Bad Guy. Or whatever.

So what's everyone else supposed to do? Just sit around and wait for the hero to show up?

Nah. That's no fun.

So I decided to write a story where our champion doesn't suffer from complacency, and decides to change the world on her own terms.

I think it's also fair to mention that subverting the Chosen One trope isn't a unique concept. Brandon Sanderson wrote an excellent "what if the Dark Lord won" story with *Mistborn*, and I'm sure that's a part of my inspiration. Will Wight wrote a great story with a non–Chosen One opposing a Dark Lord in his *Traveler's Gate* trilogy. That's one of my favorite series, so I obviously owe some of my inspiration to Will Wight as well.

But both of those cases draw more heavily from the Western tradition of the Arthurian hero, and I wanted to do something that was a little more reminiscent of the Japanese gaming heroes for franchises like *Zelda* and *Dragon Quest*.

Maoyuu Maou Yuusha is also a notable inspiration; in that story, the Hero and the Demon King decide to work together to break the cycle of violence.

(For those of you who aren't very familiar with that style, "Yui Shaw" is a pun on "Yuusha," the Japanese word for the Brave One or Hero who serves as the protagonist in that style of story. Many of my other names are similar puns—Ken Sei, for example, roughly means "Sword Saint.")

I'll also note that there were internet gaming rumors about a

AFTERWORD

Zelda game that didn't star Link that started somewhere around the *Wind Waker* era, if I remember right. So you can see those rumors as some of my inspiration, too.

Thanks to everyone who wrote the stories and made the games that helped inspire this book. I hope that this story is a worthy contribution to your legend.

ACKNOWLEDGMENTS

THERE ARE SEVERAL PEOPLE who made this story possible, not all of whom are intuitive.

Paul Lucas, my literary agent, has been a champion of my works for years now—but the original version of this book was the first he helped me negotiate. Thank you to Paul for making this book possible, as well as believing in it enough to bring the idea to traditional publishers.

Joe Monti was kind enough to give this book a shot, and I could tell from our earliest talks that he understood this story better than I could have hoped for. There's a broad history of popular media doing spins on gaming that don't quite make any sense, and I've always had to worry about publishers wanting to gut my books because they don't get the intent behind my references and jokes.

Joe was sending me Zelda references and sword videos within weeks of our first talk. Our shared background made this process *so* much easier than talks with some other publishers have been in the past—it's much easier to work with someone who actually cares about the topic.

Thanks for being an absolute delight to work with on this, Joe. Looking forward to working with you more on . . . that other thing

ACKNOWLEDGMENTS

I probably can't announce in these acknowledgments. You know what I mean.

I'd also like to thank Marc Simonetti for the fantastic cover artwork. I loved his special edition covers of *The Name of the Wind*, and I was thrilled to see his interpretation of my own book's style. I still love my original cover by LuluSeason as well—her work represents a world more like *Breath of the Wild*, whereas Marc's reminds me of the roots of my love for the series in the original *Zelda*. Thank you both.

Thank you to Steve Feldberg, my original editor at Audible, for taking a chance on the story as a whole and giving me fantastic notes. Thank you to Crystal Watanabe for the new edits for this most recent edition as well.

I also owe my thanks to Suzy Jackson and Steve West for the phenomenal audio rendition of the story, which adds a whole new layer to the tale with their fantastic performances.

A big thank-you to Bruce Rowe and Jess Richards for beta-reading the original manuscript and helping me improve the flow of this story and countless others.

Finally, thank you to Ichiro Hasegawa, a fan of the original version of the book who worked tirelessly to create a Japanese-language translation—one that is now available in audio format. I still hope we'll be able to get that translation in other formats someday, too. Thank you.

Thanks to everyone who wrote the stories and made the games that helped inspire this book. I hope that this story is a worthy contribution to your legend.

ABOUT THE AUTHOR

Andrew Rowe was once a professional game designer for awesome companies like Blizzard Entertainment, Cryptic Studios, and Obsidian Entertainment. Nowadays, he's writing full time.

When he's not crunching numbers for game balance, he runs live-action role-playing games set in the same universe as his books. In addition, he writes for pen-and-paper role-playing games.

Aside from game design and writing, Andrew watches a lot of anime, reads a metric ton of fantasy books, and plays every role-playing game he can get his hands on.

Interested in following Andrew's book releases, or discussing them with other people? You can find more info, updates, and discussions in a few places online:

Andrew's Blog: https://andrewkrowe.wordpress.com/
Mailing List: https://andrewkrowe.wordpress.com/mailing-list/
Facebook: https://www.facebook.com/Arcane-Ascension-378362729189084/
Reddit: https://www.reddit.com/r/ClimbersCourt/